Eleven Things I Promised

Also by Catherine Clark

How to Meet Boys

Unforgettable Summer

Picture Perfect

Banana Splitsville

Rocky Road Trip

Wish You Were Here

Icing on the Lake

The Alison Rules

Maine Squeeze

Love and Other Things I'm Bad At

Eleven Things I Promised

CATHERINE CLARK

HARPER TEEN

An Imprint of HarperCollinsPublishers

HarperTeen is an imprint of HarperCollins Publishers.

Eleven Things I Promised
Library of Congress Control Number: 2014959383
ISBN 978-0-06-226453-4

Typography by Lissi Erwin
16 17 18 19 20   CG/RRDH   10 9 8 7 6 5 4 3 2 1

First Edition

For my sister, who's always inspired me to do more

I was trying on a ridiculous prom dress when the call came.

I didn't even want to go to junior prom, but Stella was insisting. At the moment I was thinking of picking up a shift at McDonald's instead, just to *avoid* it, because I don't feel all that attractive in sequins and tight, fitted tube tops and flouncy things.

Those were the styles I was seeing at Flanberger's, my only retail option. If I planned on buying anything online, I'd need my mom's credit card and would have to explain why I wasn't going with Oscar and listen to her say, "It's such a shame you two aren't together anymore," for the thousandth time. (For the record, Oscar was a dirtbag, who I'd dumped after I found out he was cheating on me, like, a lot.) The concept of breaking up was somehow foreign to her, which was odd considering she'd been divorced eight years already.

Over the past week I'd become as determined as Stella to go to prom, no matter how uncomfortable it made me. Prom was a thing juniors did, whether they'd recently dumped dirtbags or not. Stella had decided she was going, that this was a thing we needed to do. Prom was the week after this big bike trip we'd signed up for—the Cure Childhood Cancer Ride—another event Stella had decided we'd do together. Of course, she was a real cyclist. I wasn't. She'd done the same ride spring of sophomore year. I hadn't.

But despite the challenges of riding so far, I couldn't wait to take off on a trip with Stella.

"We'll hit the road for a week, then we'll hit up prom. It's going to be a-mazing," she'd said as she laid out the plan in February. She was even planning to ride her bike to prom. She had it all mapped out.

She'd started outdoor training in March, as soon as the snow thawed. I hadn't. And I should have been out riding that late April afternoon with her, instead of trying to find a dress at Flanberger's. I guess I wasn't all that committed to the ride yet. I had three weeks before we left, and I knew it was time to get serious about it. Still, here I was, dress shopping. I guess

I figured Stella would pull me through the ride, the way she did with most things.

Also? Sometimes I think I was put on this earth to procrastinate.

Stella had ordered her prom dress a month ago and it was hanging in her closet.

I needed to catch up on all fronts, which is typical for me. But I had to try, because did I really want to take orders from people when they waltzed in between prom and after-prom? Would you like fries with your date? What if Oscar came in with what's her name, or what're *their* names? He would, too. He'd be clueless like that because he had no actual feelings.

Meanwhile, I'd be like Cinderella.

Literally. Sometimes I do have to mop.

No, I wasn't working prom night. I'd get a dress if it killed me, and Stella and I would go together.

"That one won't go with a rose corsage," the salesclerk, Phyllis, told me, standing back to get a good luck at the short, flowered, sequined purple dress I was currently swathed in. "Trust me."

"I don't think I'm getting a rose corsage," I said. "Trust *me*."

"Boys don't think creatively about flowers." Phyllis sounded a bit world-weary all of a sudden. "You'll be getting a rose."

"No one's doing corsages this year. We're not allowed to have the pins," I told her, not going into detail about the fact that I didn't have a guy for a date.

When Phyllis gave me a puzzled look, I added, "Potential weapons or something. They don't trust us."

"They're determined to kill prom. In my day, prom was important," Phyllis muttered. She pulled more dresses off the racks and skittered back to the dressing room with an armful. I followed her in a daze. It was like being on a Ferris wheel that you really, really wanted to get off of, but you couldn't get the attention of the ride operator to make it stop.

"Phyllis?" I murmured. "I think I need to take a break. Phyllis?"

She wasn't listening. I closed the door and prepared to change back into my own clothes.

No sooner had I started than Phyllis rapped on the door and gently threw *another* dress over the top. "Try the peach beauty on this instant," she commanded. "It will transform you."

The dress was an elaborate floor-length gown with layer upon layer of ruffles. Unfortunately, real ruffles, and not the potato chips.

No way was I wearing this, not even in a dressing room. What if there was a tornado that knocked down the entire store and I was discovered in a heap of debris with *this* thing on? Okay, so maybe tornadoes are rare in New Hampshire, but you couldn't be too careful. "No, I think I'm done," I told her. "I need to get going—"

"*Don't* walk away from this beauty," Phyllis insisted. "If you do, you'll regret it for the rest of your life. There's an old saying in women's wear. 'To peach her own.' It's a magical color."

So, now we were diving into the realm of magic. I was starting to think Phyllis needed to retire. But to humor her, I slipped out of my jeans again and pulled the dress on over my tee, not willing to commit to a full try-on. I looked at the angled neckline and how it framed my slightly round face. Something about the color did work—it wasn't one I usually wore, but it did look good against my skin.

Hold on a second. What was I thinking? The notoriously overheated Flanberger's was getting to me. *Get ahold of yourself. Those waves of fabric make you look like a curtain in a country-western furniture showroom.*

My phone rang, and I slipped it out of my purse. Stella's dad? Why was he calling? "Hello?" I said.

There was a cough, an awkward throat-clearing on the other end. "Frances, it's David Grant. Stella's been in an accident. A fairly serious accident. I wanted you to know right away."

"What—where? She . . . ?" I was already tucking my purse under my arm, lifting the latch on the changing-room door.

"The ambulance is taking her to Mercy Regional," Stella's father said. "We'll meet you there."

I shoved the phone in my purse and started pulling the dress over my head. The zipper was stuck and I couldn't get the dress off. I heard a slight tear and stopped pulling. I just grabbed my shoes, jeans, and purse and ran out of the store, past Phyllis, past the checkout, straight out into the parking lot.

At the hospital I sat beside Stella's brother, Mason. He told me she'd been on Old Route 91, out by the dairy farms where the road dips and curves. "Roller Coaster Road" was what I used to call it when I was little, and I'd scream with delight as my dad floored it to go up a steep hill and then zoom down the other side.

"So . . . who was it? Or was it a hit-and-run?"

"A woman driving a minivan hit her," Mason said. "She had two kids in the back. She called nine-one-one right away, so that's good, but . . . I don't know. I have a pretty bad feeling. Car versus bike—it's never good. What if Stella . . . you know." His voice seemed to cut out, like a lawn mower that lost its choke. He ran his hands back and forth through his short dark-brown hair, which was sticking out in various directions.

"Don't think that," I said. "She's going to be okay." I had no reason to say that, nothing to base it on, but he needed to hear it. So did I.

We'd been sitting in the waiting room together for ten minutes, and we knew Stella was conscious and being treated for pain, and she had some leg and internal injuries. That was all we knew, and it was bad enough.

We'd made small talk about Stella, the ride, Mason's freshman year at Granite State College, my stupid peach dress. The minutes were wearing on us.

Mason kept bouncing his legs up and down in a very nervous way, like he wanted to run out. Maybe he did that all the time, but if he did, I'd forgotten. I felt just as jittery. I was tapping my fingers against the chair in almost exactly the same rhythm. We were a terrible ER mariachi group. The Jitterers.

Stella's parents had been in the exam room with her ever since I'd gotten here. I'd raced through the automatic double doors in the peach chiffon nightmare of a dress. I'd planned to change when I got here but somehow misplaced my jeans between Flanberger's and Mercy. I felt so self-conscious sitting next to Mason. If it was going to take another twenty minutes until I could see Stella, then I should go find the pants.

These were the dumb things I was thinking about while I sat there on that hard red plastic seat beside Mason. It was easier to think about that than about why we were here and what was happening . . . what might be happening.

All of a sudden Mason's expression tightened. I heard footsteps in the empty hallway, coming closer. I stood up, my stomach turning somersaults, my palms sweating. A female doctor in a white coat was walking toward us, beside Stella's parents. The doctor wasn't smiling. Nobody was smiling. I wasn't breathing.

"Mom?" asked Mason. "Say something, please. Somebody."

"Stella is resting now, and she's holding her own," said the doctor. "We've stopped the blood loss and we've made her comfortable."

It sounded like something I'd heard on my mom's favorite medical drama. To my mind, "making someone comfortable" meant giving up on them—it was the horrible thing the vet had said just before he put our dog to sleep six months ago.

"We're admitting her and moving her upstairs," the doctor continued. "There are still a lot of things to sort out. She'll need some surgeries right away. . . ."

Surgeries . . . plural? She kept talking, but I somehow stopped listening. It felt like I was standing under a shower that only sprayed bad news. *Bad news. Rinse. Repeat. Bad news.* The doctor was mentioning the broken bones, the stitches on Stella's arm, how her face was bruised but was really better than it looked.

"So, can we see her now?" I asked.

"Please. I wish you would." Stella's mom put her hand on Mason's arm, which was saying a lot. Their family didn't hug much. It was just the way they were. Stella and I weren't huggers, either. We knew we were close. We didn't have to make a show of it, the way other girls ran around hugging like they hadn't seen each other for weeks when actually it was forty-five minutes between trig and chemistry.

"Stella needs to rest right now," said the doctor. "So please keep your visits short. They'll be moving her upstairs, out of ER, as quickly as it can be arranged." She nodded at Stella's parents. "I'll check in with you shortly." She strode off back down the hallway.

Mr. Grant held Mason in his gaze for a second. "You two can go visit now. I know you won't say anything upsetting, Frances. But Mason . . . just don't tell her how bad she looks. She does look pretty bad, and I know you guys always tease each other. But don't this time. Just don't."

"Right. Got it." Mason nodded, and I followed him down the hall to the exam room. "Like I'd say something right now," he muttered to me. "I mean, seriously."

"I know. You—you wouldn't." He was a very decent guy, considering he'd once gotten a video of me falling off a trampoline and shared it with the entire world. "You want to go first?" I asked him. "Or you want to go in together?"

"Actually . . . I need a drink of water first. You go ahead on your own."

I wished he hadn't said that. I didn't feel brave enough to go in by myself. "I can wait for you," I said.

"No. You go ahead. I'll be there in a minute." He looked pale and slightly ill. He had a history of puking when his family was hurt—like when Stella cut her foot on a nail in the driveway when she was five, or when their older brother dislocated his ankle doing a skateboard trick. It was almost sort of cute, or would be if it didn't involve throwing up. I decided not to push him.

When I walked into Stella's hospital room, I felt a wave of anxiety nearly knock me over. The floor was wobbly. My legs were shaking. I wished Mason had come in beside me so I'd have someone to fall onto.

I surveyed the room, not wanting to look at Stella, which was crazy. I had to look, had to go comfort her. I was scared out of my mind. Her hands were wrapped in gauze, and her elbow was taped. She had one long, bright-red scrape on her chin, covered in ointment—it was stitches, I saw as I got closer. She had tons of small wounds on her face, probably gravel driven into her skin. Her blue eyes looked glassy, and at the same time, washed out.

I took a moment to compose myself. The last thing she needed was to see me freak out. She was going to be fine. She was banged up, sure, and she'd be on crutches for a while, but she was going to be okay.

"You look terrible," I suddenly blurted.

"Thanks," she muttered.

"I'm sorry, Stells. I'm really sorry I said that." Oh God. Why was I such an idiot at times? "I guess . . . it's a law for best friends to be honest, isn't it? Plus, I kind of panicked."

Stella took a long, slow breath and winced. "In that case," she said slowly, "that dress is hideous."

"I know, right? I was trying on prom dresses when your dad called and—anyway, how are you feeling?"

"I can't feel anything, actually," she said. "I guess I'm drugged up on painkillers."

"I'm sorry. I'm so sorry about what happened," I said.

"Quit saying sorry," she said. "It was fun while it lasted. We were going to prom. We were going to do the Cure Ride.

And now nothing," she said in a flat voice.

"Don't say *nothing*! We can still go to prom, we can still . . ." My voice trailed off. "Do lots of things." I perched on a chair beside the bed. She looked exhausted, with dark lines under her eyes, as if she hadn't slept in a few days. Bedsheets and white blankets covered her midsection, but tubes ran underneath the covers, connected to monitors, making clicking noises periodically with her vital signs.

She was pulling at a thread on the top blanket. "They gave me this stupid warming blanket," she said, "like it'll help." Tears trickled out the sides of her eyes. I grabbed a tissue and started to hand it to her, then realized she wasn't up to using her arms much. I'd need to do the work. I dabbed at the tears rolling down her cheeks. This was such a backward situation. She never cried. She was usually the one who handed *me* Kleenex. I fell apart at sad movies and pet stores and random other places.

Stella fiddled with the plastic hospital ID bracelet on her left wrist. When her fingers touched the IV tube in the back of her hand, she pulled her hand away. "I hate these things."

"I've never had one," I said. "Does it hurt?"

"Not exactly. More like it feels like you're trapped." We both contemplated that for a minute, me staring at her pinched skin, the heavy tape and plastic tube, and her looking anywhere but her hand. I looked up at the liquid dripping down the tube from a couple of plastic pouches, pulsing into her.

The door opened behind us, and I glanced over my shoulder to see Mrs. Grant walk in. Stella's mom walked over and laid her hand on my shoulder. "Franny, do you think you could go to our house and pack a bag for Stella? You'd know what she wants, and that way, we can stay here."

"Sure—sure, I'll do that. No problem." I knew they were probably trying to get rid of me for a while, and though it made me feel guilty to think this way, there was a part of me that was all right taking a break. Stella looked so unlike herself. It was almost as if I didn't know this Stella. I jumped up and started for the door, then turned back to take a last glance at Stella. "I'll be back later, okay?"

She didn't answer. I wasn't sure if she was asleep or if she just didn't hear me.

I headed out into the hallway and nearly bumped into Mason. He was holding a bundle of blue fabric.

"These jeans belong to you? I found them in the parking lot."

I couldn't respond.

"You said . . . you lost them? I went outside to get some fresh air by my truck and, well. I saw these crumpled on the pavement like someone dropped them."

The floor seemed to fall away underneath me, and I felt like I was losing my balance, plunging, arms outstretched, reaching for the ground as if I were in an elevator that was crashing.

"You don't look good." Mason grabbed onto my waist, forcing me to lean against him. "You feeling all right?"

"Not . . ." I couldn't find the words. I couldn't figure out what to do. I knew I should sit down, but I didn't know where to find a chair.

He took my arm and guided me to a chair by the nurses' station. "Sit down for a minute. Sit right here. Head down, Franny. Breathe slowly."

I leaned over, head between my legs, eyes facing the shiny hospital floor. I hugged the jeans as if they were my favorite blanket. My warming blanket.

"Come on, Frances. It's going to be okay." Mason crouched down beside me and rubbed my back once or twice.

Easy for him to say. He hadn't seen her yet.

I must be crazy. That was all I could think as a white, slightly dented van from Rocco's Ink Den pulled up in front of my house at seven in the morning. *I'm not really about to do this, am I?*

This was different when Stella and I planned on doing it together.

Her parents were going to drive us to the start in Bangor, Maine. The ride went from there along coastal Maine through New Hampshire and then finished in Boston. Stella'd had it all figured out. How we wouldn't have to hang out with our school bike group all the time, because a few of them were pretty annoying. How after the ride we'd spend a day or two in Boston being tourists and recovering. But now it was just me, standing by my driveway with my mom, who, no joke, was wearing a robe and slippers because it was Sunday and she didn't have to get ready for work.

A lot had happened since Stella's accident, but the upshot of it was that I was headed off on the seven-day, three-hundred-fifty-mile Cure Childhood Cancer Ride without her.

The van's passenger door opened, and Max Modella climbed out. "You ready?" he asked. Max, with his shoulder-length hair and muscular, tattooed arms, looked more like a twenty-five-year-old than one of my classmates. I guess that's what happens when your uncle owns the tattoo parlor in town.

He could make a plain white T-shirt look hot, the way underwear models do. That's all I know. Something about his angular nose and cheekbones. He had about a dozen girl-friends at school; I couldn't keep track of who was current. His uncle Rocco had offered to drive us to the ride's start, and since he had a full-size van and a trailer that could hold our eight bikes, we'd accepted.

"Hey. Your hair?" Max asked. "Was it like that before?"

I wheeled my bike toward Max, declining to answer the question. As of this morning at about one a.m., my hair was bleached blond. Two days before, it had been lightish brown, which went a lot better with my lightish-brown skin.

Max was a laid-back guy who tended not to keep up on the details. Once our American history class moved classrooms, and he didn't catch on until halfway through the term. He kept going to the old room, the way a dog will do if you move across town.

"Well, can we have your stuff?" he asked. "Blondie?"

"Don't call me that," I told him as I followed him to the bike trailer. I tried to lift the bike into it, but I got it only as far as my shoulders. The trailer was way too tall for me. While I was struggling to lift the bike higher—it really didn't weigh that much, which made it even more embarrassing that I was about to be crushed—Max lifted it easily out of my hands.

"I'll take it from here," Max said.

"Thanks," I said.

"Blondie," he added again.

I shook my head, grabbed my duffel and sleeping bag, and stowed them in the back of the van, jamming them in on top of everyone else's. My bike helmet was attached to the duffel bag's handles, a shocking neon green that nobody could miss. Kind of like my new hair color.

Now what? I'd asked the mirror as I stood there, water dripping onto my shoulders. *Do I have to bleach my eyebrows to match? Or . . . anywhere else?*

I hurried back to say a quick good-bye to my mom. She'd

packed a giant cooler full of snacks for the team. She'd stayed up half the night baking granola bars and brownies and muffins. I knew, because I'd stayed up just as long, packing and repacking. She was so tired she hadn't even commented on my hair except to say, "Hm, nice, you can do that sort of thing when you're young."

I had to give Mom credit. For someone who really didn't want me to go on this trip, she was being very supportive.

"Here, I got you something. The girl at the Bike Barn said it's the one thing every cyclist should have." She handed me a small paper bag, and I pulled out a complicated gizmo with about a dozen different levers and functions.

"So what does this do?" I asked, turning the metal tool over and over in my hand.

"It's a wrench? I don't know," she said. "I really have no idea. I asked for a recommendation." She laughed and gave me a hug. I had to try really, really hard not to cry. I'm terrible at good-byes, and looking at the tears running down my mother's cheeks, I had a good idea where I'd inherited that trait.

"Mom, it's going to be fine," I said, brushing my eyes. "*We're* fine."

"I know—but—but—" she stammered as she sobbed.

"You said butt," I told her, which got her to laugh. "You said but-but, actually. Which seems like as good a time as any for me to leave." I gave her another quick hug. "Promise me you'll check in on Stells for me."

"I will. And you, be safe," she said as I turned around to climb into the van. I knew what she meant. *Stay on the side of the road. Way, way over. Look out for cars. Don't let the same thing happen to you that happened to Stella.*

Inside the van, Autumn Daye (yes, that's her real name) and Alex Nelson were sitting in the very back row, all wrapped around each other, as per usual. Not only were they never apart, they were the typical football player/cheerleader combination. It was like they were following a script.

Margo Maloney—my archnemesis since we fought over the same doll stroller at preschool—Will Oxendale, and Elsa Stevenson were in the third-row seat. Cameron Cruz sat on the small second-row seat where I was to join him.

They all stared at me. "Uh, morning," I said. "Ignore my mom and her robe." I perched on the bench seat, holding my small bag close to me.

Cameron waved hello, while simultaneously nodding to the music he was listening to through white earbuds. Autumn and Alex glanced up at me, then went back to snuggling and talking about their plans for high school domination. Typical. They were the power couple at Sparrowsdale High. I was just a regular person.

"What did you do to your hair?" demanded Margo, wrinkling her tiny nose. She really did have the most perfect nose on the planet. And small ears, too. She reminded me of a chipmunk. Tiny, quick, and hyperactive.

"I like your hair," said Will. "I think it's rather avant-garde. A bit cheeky, even." He was from England, an exchange student for spring term, and his British accent made him sound smarter than the rest of us. Trust me. We were in English Lit together, and if he raised his hand to make the exact same comment I did, somehow he'd get an "Exactly!" and I wouldn't.

"It's nothing. Don't mention it, actually," I said, lowering my shoulders, wanting to shrink for a minute.

"Well, why did you do it if you didn't want people to notice it?" Margo asked.

"Oh, I just felt like it," I said. It was a long story, one I wasn't about to go into with her. Though we'd supposedly been friends for a minute when we were in preschool (before the doll stroller incident), we'd never liked each other, even though we were on the same dance team, the Shooting Sparks, for two years. We hadn't spoken much at all since we both outgrew the team. Margo had her friends, and I had mine. Mostly, I had Stella.

"Never mind. I thought Stella was going to come see us

off," Margo said, leaning forward and looking around the yard, as if Stella would be hiding in the bushes outside my house or something.

"Oh, she was going to. She planned on it," I lied. "But then she got a last-minute doctor's appointment this morning."

"At seven?" Margo scoffed.

"It's an, uh, it's an MRI. For her leg. To see how it's healing. They do those early, I guess." I shrugged. I was used to making excuses for her. I'd been saying things like, *She's self-conscious about her facial injuries*, and *She has a meeting with the police today to reconstruct the accident*, and *Her parents are being really protective and won't let her go out.*

None of them were true.

The truth was, her injuries were a lot more serious than she wanted anyone to know. She wouldn't *want* to be here to see off this group.

"I'm pretty sure they can do MRIs any time of day," Margo replied. "My brother broke his foot and he had one right away—"

"What do you want me to say? I'm not her doctor," I snapped. "How should I know why they scheduled it at seven?"

"Fine. I was only asking. I'm just concerned," said Margo, sitting back between Will and Elsa. "Don't bite my head off."

Too late, I thought. I turned around and faced forward, my blood pounding. Why did Margo have to pry? Then again, that was the way she was—obnoxious. Of course Stella wanted to be here, way, way deep down. But she was barely speaking to me or to anybody. There was no way she was ready to be a cheerleader for the team she'd started, organized, and now couldn't be on.

Since I'd stepped up and become a real team member instead of just Stella's tagalong friend, I'd gotten to know the team a little bit better—but not much. We'd posed for pictures, we'd sent hundreds of texts, we'd trotted around school and our neighborhoods, begging for donations and pledges. We'd even spent an entire Saturday afternoon at the supermarket, bagging groceries and asking for donations. Despite all that, we hadn't exactly *bonded*.

In fact, some people had gotten really competitive about the bagging. It was annoying. Margo started campaigning the minute someone stepped into the store—"Pick me! Check out in lane three!"—and Autumn and Alex were no better, acting like the Homecoming Queen and King they were.

I was a better bagger—before my McDonald's job, I worked one summer at a pharmacy where I bagged plenty of odd-shaped stuff—but *they* got all the customers.

Life. So unfair.

Cameron leaned over from his spot against the window. "You know what I realized when we picked you up?" he asked. "Our house matches yours. Same colors. Same size, everything."

"Really? You live in the same development?" I asked.

"Oh, yeah. I live in Sector Ten. Otherwise known as Landing Lane. It's a copy of your block, right down to the mailbox stripes. It's so fake." He shook his head. "It kills me."

I laughed. "I know," I agreed. "It's like a set for a really boring movie."

"Revenge of the Vacuum Cleaner. Crime in the Cul-de-Sac," Cameron said.

I laughed again. Cameron was a funny writer—I knew that from working on yearbook with him. Not that yearbook was my thing, exactly. I was just following orders to get involved in activities for my college applications.

I didn't think working on yearbook and working at McDonald's was going to score me any points, though. I'd have to kick it up a notch over the summer and fall semester of senior year. I was so dreading that. I liked my little noninvolved world.

Cameron held out a small bag toward me. "Try one? They're protein-and-carb cubes. Great for energy."

"Oh, um, sure." I recognized the brand as one that Stella

liked, too. I'd take all the help I could get. I popped one into my mouth and chewed slowly, the lemonade-glazed gel glob dissolving in my mouth. It was horrible. How did anyone eat these? I took a sip from my water bottle to wash the bad taste out of my mouth. "How long until we get to Bangor?"

Cameron glanced at his phone. "Three hours. Enjoy." He slipped his earbuds back in and closed his eyes, leaning his head against the window. He definitely was not a morning person. When we'd had first-period biology together, he often ran in fifteen minutes late and would have to clean up after labs to make up for it, so Mr. Bamford wouldn't report him to the main office. I don't think he cared about having to do clean-up. He seemed to think it was a fair trade for getting to come in late.

I looked out the window, feeling the familiar pang I got whenever I left town.

We crossed the roads where I'd gone on training rides over the past few weeks—some with Mason, and some by myself. He was always patient about the fact that I was slow on hills (well, slow everywhere, actually), even though it must have driven him crazy to wait for me. He'd ride to the top, then coast down beside me and climb once more, but at my pace. He never said anything critical, unless it was about the dumb things Stella and I did when we were little, or the fact that I wore jeans and long-sleeved shirts for rides.

I didn't feel comfortable wearing all that cycling gear. It just highlighted how much I wasn't a real cyclist yet, unlike the rest of them. It also meant I nearly drowned in my own sweat once or twice.

I'd since forced myself to buy a couple of pairs of long biking shorts that had a padded liner so my butt wouldn't hurt after the first ten miles—but they weren't the skin-tight look; that was just the inner layer. The outer layer was baggy and black. Along with those, I had on a bike jersey, and in a small bag next to me were Stella's old clip-on shoes, which she was lending me. We wore the same size, which was lucky. In the meantime I was wearing flip-flops.

I gazed at the river we were crossing, where a rower in a single scull was headed upstream, oars cutting through the early-morning fog that hung over the water.

Stella and I had canoed the same river the summer before. We'd packed a lunch, planned the place where her dad would pick us up, and drifted downstream blasting music from our phones and singing along. We'd gotten sunburned, eaten by mosquitoes, and nearly swamped by a powerboat full of men who whistled at us until we told them we were sixteen and paddled quickly to shore.

It had been the best day of the whole summer.

Now, I reached into my jersey's back pocket for my phone, hoping against hope that Stella had sent me an encouraging "good-bye and good luck" text.

Nope.

I'd just barely been allowed to visit her and say good-bye the night before.

"So you're really going," she'd said in a flat voice.

"Well, yeah. I told you I would. Maybe I don't always follow through on things, but this time I'm going to," I said. "I promised you, right?"

She shrugged. "I don't know. Did you?"

She had acted as if she had no memory of this, when I'd told her at least five times that I would do the ride for her and wouldn't bail no matter what happened. I'd promised her I'd do it without letting anyone know how badly hurt she was, too. Either she didn't remember some of our conversations in the hospital, or else she didn't care enough to pay attention.

This wasn't how it was supposed to be. We should have been traveling together; if we were, we'd have been packing our bags at each other's houses and laughing and imagining all the ridiculous things that might happen on the trip. We'd have packed too many things. We'd have stayed up too late and crashed in her parents' minivan the next morning on the way to the start.

But there wasn't any of that. There was only a weird interaction with her not making eye contact, not looking up, staring out the window. She was suffering, and I couldn't help her.

"So I hope everything goes okay while I'm gone," I'd said to her. "And I'll make sure I get pictures of all the team so you can see how things go on the ride."

She didn't say anything.

When I finally made it out the door, crying, Mason had run after me. "Sorry. She just . . . she's not herself," he said.

"She hates me," I said.

"Don't take it personally. She hates everything right now," he said.

"I can't *blame* her. I would, too. I'd probably hate me, too, but I'm really doing this for her."

"Try to have a good time if you can, and don't freak out. You'll be fine."

"If you consider fine crashing and totaling my bike, then yeah," I joked.

He looked a bit shocked by my choice of words, and his face reddened as he stopped beside me, flustered.

"No, I—God, I'm sorry," I said. "I didn't mean—"

"I know," he said quickly. "I know you didn't."

We'd been spending so much time together that we were

beginning to understand each other. We were both trying to get Stella past this awful stage, these terrible weeks. We both knew that some of what Stella's parents were saying and doing was driving her—and us—crazy. They wouldn't let any of us out of their sight without huge promises and explanations. Mason and I had both been covering for Stella, making sure she was all alone for as long as she wanted to be, but not so alone that she got lonely or desperate.

The night was so silent. I could hear frogs in the pond behind their house, peeping so loudly that it seemed they must be having conversations.

"Sorry. I'm so stupid." I shook my head. "Some things aren't funny anymore."

"Lots of things," added Mason. "Actually."

I nodded, brushing my wet eyes with my fingers, trying to pull it together.

"Don't worry about the ride, or being gone for a week. Stella will be fine, and you'll do okay. You are kind of in shape."

"Kind of? Thanks," I said, shoving him.

"Now it's time to take your little wings and fly." Mason patted me on the head like I was a toddler, the way he always did when he wanted to aggravate me. He was only two years older, but at times he tried to make it seem as if it were five.

I brushed his hand away, but instead of letting go, we both held on for a few seconds. It felt odd, but at the same time comfortable. "There will be no flying, okay?"

Mason and I looked at each other like: *Are we supposed to hug good-bye now or something?* Because we didn't usually hug, unless it was a tackling move when we were in elementary school and we all fought like cats and dogs over swords and lightsabers.

"We used to always say this thing when I was on the track team at Sparrowsdale. I think of it when I go running. It's kind of annoying, but my coach would always say, 'Fly like you mean it.' So, fly like you mean it, Frances." Mason let go of my hand, gave me a fist bump, and then walked away.

I'd felt super sad as I looked back at the house, the chili pepper mini-lights that would normally be in Stella's room, but were now on the first floor, in the den, which was her bedroom for the time being. It was like a hospital room inside a house. She was still in recovery mode, and nobody could say how much longer it might take. "Her incisions practically have incisions," was what her father had told me the last time I visited. "I don't want her risking an infection. We'll have to be patient."

I didn't know how to ask him how patient I had to be in terms of her coming back to me, to school, to . . . everything.

◆◆◆

Now, in front of me, Max opened his window, and the vanilla fragrance tree hanging above my seat blew in the breeze, spinning like a whirling dervish. I tried not to look at it, but it was impossible. The more I watched it, the dizzier I felt. I don't do well in multiple-passenger vehicles. I don't.

"Stop the van," I said to Max's uncle Rocco. "Stop!"

He pulled over onto the shoulder of the highway, to safety, and I flung open the door. I stumbled out of the van and down into a slight ravine, where the protein cube and half a cup of coffee quickly left me.

Glamorous.

This wasn't the beginning I'd planned. We were only thirty miles in—not even on bikes—and I was already not making it.

I pulled a stick of gum from the pack in my shorts pocket and took a minute to make sure I was really all right. Then I headed up the embankment to the van.

"Don't tell me the whole trip is going to be like this," Margo said.

She really had a great bedside—or vanside—manner. So caring.

"You okay?" Will asked, leaning out of the van. "Do you need a Pepto? I've got some tablets in my bag."

I figured he was talking about the notoriously pink Pepto-Bismol. "I'll be okay," I said. "I think."

"Sorry," Cameron said. "Next time, skip the protein cube, maybe?" He leaned over and pulled the flying fragrance tree off the string where it was hanging with one snap. He stuffed it into a side pocket beside him.

"Agreed," I told him as I stood outside, taking one last breath before getting back into the van.

"Hangover?" asked Max, leaning out the front window.

"*What?*" I said. "No. Motion sickness."

"Here, sit in the front," said Max, climbing out onto the shoulder of the highway. "You won't feel half as sick up there."

I peered in at the empty seat. Rocco, the driver, patted the seat with his hand, which was completely covered in colorful tattoos—just like his nephew Max's arms. "Come on, I won't bite."

"Oh." I laughed. "I know."

Someone tapped my shoulder, and I turned around. "Here." Margo was leaning forward, a plastic grocery bag in her hand. "Use this if it happens again so we don't have to pull over and lose time."

I balled up the plastic bag and stuffed it into the console between the front seats. Oh, yeah. This was going to be a great trip.

After a minute, I pulled a small green piece of paper out of my pocket and unfolded it.

I'd found this list that day when I went to Stella's room to get some things for her. It was sitting on her desk, beside her laptop, as if she'd been working on it earlier that day. Before the car crashed into her.

After, I'd gone back to get it.

I wouldn't tell her I had the list or that I was planning to complete it for her—unless and until it turned out well.

From the Desk of . . . Stella Artois Grant (SAG)
The Junior Year Bike Trip F(ix)-It List
aka What I Promise I Will Do While
Raising Money to Find a Cure for Childhood
Cancer, Because My Life Needs Fixing Too.
Not Necessarily in This Order

1. Bleach my hair blond.
2. Dance with one of the Sparrowsdale guys on the trip.
3. Leave an anonymous $100 gift for an unexpected kindness.
4. Start a food fight.
5. Ride in my bikini one day; swim in my bike clothes the next.

6. Drink a beer or a vodka drink or something stronger than water.
7. Dance in the rain and sleep under the stars. Or vice versa, but sleeping in the rain would not be fun.
8. Get my belly button pierced. Seriously.
9. Ride the Devil's Drop of Doom at Phantom Park.
10. Have an epic kiss.

For weeks, Stella had been talking about some of the things she wanted to do on the trip, all the things she'd do differently this year. She'd said how she wanted to take more risks. "I usually just ride and read and hang out in the tent. I eat right, I get enough sleep, and all that boring stuff that makes my parents happy but doesn't really make me happy. So this year, I wanted to pull out all the stops and push myself. I promised myself. Now that you're doing the trip, too, I'm counting on you to help me pull them off."

"Sure, sure," I'd told her at the time. "Anything you want."

"Seriously?" Stella had stared openmouthed at me in shock.

"No, of course not!" I cried. "I can't do this stuff."

"Where there's a list, there's a way," Stella said. "I'll make a list. You follow it with me."

"This sounds like those New Year's resolutions you made for us freshman year. Remember how *that* turned out?"

Somehow our list of resolutions had fallen out of her backpack and into the wrong hands. Henry Wooster's. He was on the list of "People We'll Get to Know Better. Way Better."

Stella had paused at the memory, but only for a second. "It's because of the Henry Wooster incident that I learned never to put anything super specific on a list. So don't worry. There are no names on it," she said.

Still, every time I read the list, I got this awful, uneasy feeling. I wasn't the person to carry out this list. I was (a) a chicken, (b) afraid of heights and rides that involved heights, and (c) not keen on public displays of my nearly naked body. In fact, I'd pretty much rather die than do a few of these things.

I had pierced ears, sure, but I wasn't that interested in poking more holes in my skin.

And drinking alcohol wasn't something I'd planned on attempting until age 21, at least. My family didn't have a good history with that, according to my mother, who had lectured me many times on the dangers of drinking, always bringing up the example of a long-lost uncle of mine. Perhaps it would count if I just took a sip of something; a sip couldn't kill me, right?

The Devil's Drop of Doom, on the other hand, totally could.

I was crazy to take on this ride and the F(ix)-It List. In fact, I was already calling it the F-It List because of my attitude toward some of the items on it. But if checking things off this list for Stella would help her in any way, at all, I would do it. I just wasn't sure how. Maybe I could drink *before* the ride. In large quantities. I hadn't been on a roller coaster since I was ten, when I was petrified and screamed so loudly that I lost my voice for a week afterward.

I casually looked over my shoulder at everyone. Which one of these guys could I possibly dance with? And did Stella put that on the list because she wanted to dance with either Will, Alex, Cameron, or Max? I didn't think any of them were exactly her type—at least, she hadn't mentioned having any interest in anyone in particular.

Maybe she had a crush on Max; that I could see. But he wasn't her type; she was way more on the straight and narrow. He was notorious for two things: flirting and partying.

Alex was taken, which was okay. He had one of those block-style heads, or maybe it was that his neck was too thick and so it was all one unit. He could be on steroids. I don't know.

Then there was Cameron, my neighbor and seeming slouchster. (There was a shoe shop in town called Shoester, and Stella and I pretty much applied the phrasing to anyone and anything we could.) I thought he was cute and witty, but he wasn't Stella's type.

That left Will Oxendale, the tallest, string-beaniest person in our school—I didn't know him well at all, since he had only arrived in town in January, but the fact that he only wore soccer and bike jerseys day after day made him a bit boring. Day one: cool. Day twenty-one: not cool.

As for the epic kiss . . . I glanced in the mirror on the sunshade above me, adjusting it slightly so I could see myself. Gazing up at my now-blond hair, I hardly recognized myself. I turned slightly and pursed my lips as I applied sunscreen lip balm. Did I look more kissable as a platinum blond, or was it just me?

Suddenly I noticed another face in the mirror. It was Max, sitting directly behind me. Our eyes met.

I immediately flipped up the shade and went back to staring out the window.

Awkward.

Forget boys. I'd kiss my bike when I finished. That would be epic.

CHAPTER 2

We arrived at the starting point just north of Bangor, Maine, about three and a half hours later and parked on a large open field, the trailer and van bouncing and jostling as we drove over bumpy ground. I couldn't believe how many vans, people, and bikes there were. The other thirty-nine high school teams who were registered could have filled up a football field and then some.

Stella ought to be here. I couldn't help thinking it. I didn't feel right being here without her.

She'd pulled me through all the rough times. Freshman year, around the same time I quit dance team, we both had this notoriously difficult Current Events and Politics teacher, who gave us a homework assignment that involved so much research I felt buried by all the library books and websites we had to consult.

I ran into Stella at the library one afternoon. She looked very organized. "I don't know how to do this project," I confessed. "I don't have a clue."

"Well, what country did you get?" she asked.

"I've got Costa Rico," I said.

She laughed. "Rica, you mean?"

"Costco Rico?" I asked. "Whatever." We both started laughing harder and couldn't stop; we got so loud we were yelled at by the librarian. More than once.

We weren't supposed to get or give help on this assignment. But we did, anyway.

It was the first time I felt completely stonewalled by a homework assignment, and I ended up with a B. Stella got an A, as per usual.

Since this class was one of our "core competency" deals, I had to score a B or better in order to get credit. I'd never have made it to the next level without Stella's help on the report. In fact, she'd helped me navigate almost all of high school so far. Basically, I owed her my life. Or at least my diploma, when I got it.

◆◆◆

Margo and Oxendale headed to the registration tent to check us in while we unloaded the trailer and found where we should put our bags. We'd ride that afternoon and camp that night, so our bags were going right into another truck and trailer.

We each had to bring one sleeping bag, one duffel bag, one bike, and associated gear, like of course helmets, water bottles, a patch kit, an extra tire tube. But if anything bad happened, I was relying on the so-called sag wagon (a fancy cycling term for a support van) to save me. The ride had mechanics. I didn't need to become one, too. Stella was usually my mechanic, to be honest. She'd fill up the tires and oil the chain on my bike and then shout, "Follow me!" as she took off down the street. An experienced racer, she'd won a few first-place finishes in her age group at bigger time-trial events. She'd even had a bike shop who wanted to sponsor her, put their name on her jersey.

Stella had switched to cycling when she had one too many concussions from playing soccer. She was crushed when she had to give up soccer, because she was so good. Cycling was supposed to be her "safe" sport. It could make me ill if I thought about it for too long.

As soon as we'd got our bikes and gear unloaded, Rocco announced he was hitting the road, back to Sparrowsdale.

Wait a second, I wanted to say. *Don't rush off. Do you think you could pierce my belly button first?*

But I had no privacy here. So instead, I thanked him for the ride, just like everyone else did. "No problem. Needed to pick up some supplies over here anyway. Ride like the wind, my friends," he said, giving us a little salute.

Max shook his head. "Uncle Rock, don't go quoting bad songs."

"I'm serious," Rocco said, laughing. "Ride with the wind at your back."

Margo rolled her eyes, as if that were the stupidest thing she'd ever heard. "We don't exactly get to *choose* the direction of the wind."

"Still. It's a well-known Irish blessing, that's what you're thinking of," said Will. "May the road rise up to meet you. May the wind always be at your back."

"If the road rises up to meet me, I think I'll crash," I joked.

"Or, you know, throw up," said Margo.

I glared at her, wondering when she was going to let it go. A person gets sick now and then.

Max put his hand on my shoulder and I tried not to flinch. With his tattooed arms, chains, and height, he was a bit intimidating. "You'll be fine. It's like—well, I was going to say it's like riding a bike. You have to get back on. But you'll already be on it."

"Deep," Cameron teased him. "Dude, that's so deep I just fell in."

Rocco climbed into the van and leaned out the window. "Call me with details the night before you guys finish. I'll be there to pick you up in Boston, unless you make other plans."

We thanked him again for the ride and then watched him drive away, the bike trailer bouncing and clattering across the field. I didn't think anyone would say it, but we were kind of like the country bumpkins here. Other teams came from Boston; Portland, Maine; and Portsmouth, New Hampshire, to name a few. We were the Sparrowsdale Mighty Sparrows, from a small town north of North Conway, which sounds like "double north," not that it's something you can double. Extra-north, maybe?

Mighty Sparrows. Since when has a sparrow ever intimidated anyone? They might as well have called us the baby birds, or the downy chicks.

We headed from the parking area to the gazebo and picnic tables. There was a lunch buffet spread out, and although I was feeling a lot better, I didn't necessarily want to grab a sandwich anytime soon. I stood off to the side, debating.

"You should eat," Margo said as she walked past me. "You'll bonk early if you don't eat."

"I know." I nodded. "I should."

"You always liked bananas. Eat one of those and pack one for later," she said.

Why are you giving me good advice? And why do you even remember that? I wanted to ask. "I liked bananas when I was four. I haven't actually liked them since," I told her.

"Suit yourself," she said. "They'll really help with not cramping up."

I took a banana and went to sit in the grass beside Cameron. Because I felt I knew him better than anyone else in the group, I was glomming on to him like peanut butter onto bread. Like me, he didn't exactly look like a high-powered athlete, but it was hard to tell when he was sitting next to Will Oxendale—whom everyone called by his last name, for some reason. Oxendale was about a foot taller than him, and his legs reminded me of a flamingo. A very muscular flamingo.

Meanwhile, the trip director, Heather, was giving a welcome speech to the crowd from a microphone on the little gazebo. She greeted everyone, then started to go over the rules and regulations. While every rider had raised a certain amount already, there would be new and different speed challenges every morning; the first three riders to finish would get a thousand dollars donated to their team total, thanks to various sponsors.

While I listened, I mentally reviewed Stella's F-It List. I

was pretty sure that almost half of her list was against the rules. Not only would I need luck to finish each day's ride, I'd need luck not to get caught.

Half an hour later, it was time to line up behind the wide ribbon. The area around the start was beginning to get completely congested as people got ready. It had quickly filled with swarms of bicycles, riders, course officials, and volunteers rushing around to get everything set.

I hurried over to the pavilion to fill up my two water bottles. I found our assigned table where my duffel still sat and slipped off my flip-flops and put on Stella's cycling shoes, fastening the Velcro straps over the tops. GO FRANCES GO was written in capital letters on masking tape on the straps.

Inside the shoe was a note, sort of like a fortune cookie, only one that smelled like shoe instead of sugar. I unfolded the note. The handwriting wasn't Stella's.

You know how to do this. And you're ready. Just keep pedaling.
—Mason

I felt this nervous flutter when I saw his name. Mason had run a couple of time trials for me a few days ago, and although I was pretty sure he'd rigged them, or forgotten to start the time right away, it had helped me mentally get ready to be around *this* many riders.

I took a photo of the shoes and posted it, tagging both Mason and Stella. *Ready to start the Cure Childhood Cancer Ride!* I took a selfie with my ride number and name attached to my shirt and quickly posted that as well. I was glad I had a number. That way, if anything happened, some random person driving by and finding me sitting on the side of the road could identify me to the ride organizers—you know, because I'd probably be incoherent at that point.

I delivered my duffel to the bag drop and headed to the starting line with my bike—Stella's bike, technically. Her family had insisted I use it, because my own bike wasn't exactly on the same level. It was more of a discount-store purchase, while this bike was one Stella had used before she got a custom one. It had a lot of miles on it, but still looked new and sleek. It was probably way too good for me, a novice rider, but I loved how lightweight it was and how it caught the sunlight on its silver-blue frame.

I found an open spot in the middle-to-back part of the crowd. I adjusted my helmet and straddled the bike. Thirty miles. This was going to be the easiest of all seven days. So why was my stomach tied in knots? Stupid protein cubes. If anyone ever offers you something you've never eaten before, as you (a) ride in a multipassenger vehicle or (b) start a major athletic undertaking? Just. Say. No.

"Welcome, once again, to the ninth annual Cure Childhood Cancer Ride!" Heather was sitting atop a tall ladder under the Start Here banner. "We're so glad to have all of you riding today. I want to thank you for your contributions. Together we can beat this thing!"

We all cheered and whooped. I felt a shiver go down my spine. I'd never been part of something this big, for such a good cause, before. Contributing fifty dollars to Stella's ride last year didn't really count. Neither did the dollar I threw into the Salvation Army kettle at Christmas.

"Is everybody ready?" Heather counted down from ten, and everyone around me was chanting, too. "Three-two-one . . . bike!" we all screamed.

I pushed off gingerly and tried to avoid ramming into anyone as I settled into the seat. "Step one," Mason had coached me, "is stay on the bike."

My wheels were nearly touching the wheels of the girl's bike in front of me, and her wheels were almost on top of the guy's wheels in front of *her*. I thought we were in for a long, awkward ride, until faster riders separated off the front of the pack, the middle spread out, and the rest of us settled into the back.

I kept my head down as I gained speed, getting into a good spot. I didn't want to be last. If I started out in last place, there was no telling where I'd end up. Probably I'd never make it out of third gear. I might not even make it out of Bangor.

I shifted quickly to higher gears, getting more comfortable as I focused on the road ahead. My muscles responded, settling into a good, sustained pace. Not everyone here was trying to set a speed record. There were at least a few dozen riders going my pace. *Easy peasy,* I thought, repeating something Oxendale had said in the van when we went over the instructions for our first day. *Easy peasy, lemon squeezy.*

Speaking of Oxendale, I thought I spotted him up ahead. I tried to ride fast enough to catch up with him, but it was impossible. The faster I rode, the farther ahead he seemed to get. Not surprising. Suddenly Oxendale (or whoever it was) kicked up his pace a notch and zoomed to the front, like he'd just added an electric motor to his bike.

Where were Cameron, Max, and the inseparable couple? Where was Margo? In a pack this big, we were going to need something more to keep track of one another—matching shirts or stickers, something bold and neon. This team might be great at athletics, but they were terrible at teamwork-type stuff. Maybe that was one of the pieces Stella normally brought to the group. Without her, we were just eight individuals; that is, if you counted Autumn and Alex as individuals.

I thought back to the day I walked into our weekly team check-in meeting to tell everyone that Stella wouldn't make it, that her leg was badly broken, but that I'd still be riding with them.

They looked at me as if I were insane. As if they only wanted me if I were part of the package deal. They were all experienced cyclists, most of whom had done this same charity ride the year before. They planned on doing the sprint challenges every day, racing one another to the finish line, whereas I just had my sights set on finishing each segment. That'd be enough of a challenge for me.

The more I thought about Stella, and her not being here, the harder I rode. I started passing a couple of people. Then a few more. Each time I reached a faster mph speed, the little computer on my handlebars beeped.

I was looking down at it when suddenly I was crossing train tracks and my front wheel slid sideways a bit as my back wheel slid another way—the bike bobbled but I kept my balance, pushing hard on the handlebars and recovering into a straight but wobbly line. *Phew*, I thought as I glanced down to check the computer and try to get back up to speed.

That's when my front tire hit a deep pothole. I went flying over the handlebars, landing on my butt, scraping my wrist on the pavement as I bounced to the side of the road.

Whoever said blondes have more fun had obviously never gone on a mass bike ride.

I got up right away and brushed off the dirt and grit. It was only a few scratches and some missing skin. I'd have bruises tomorrow. Big ones.

Please, I thought, *let nobody be looking at me*.

"Hey, you okay?" Three different people stopped to check on me. "You want a Band-Aid? I've got one." "Ouch. I hate when I hit potholes."

"I know, right?" I laughed, despite the fact that my road burn was starting to throb a little. "No, I'm okay."

"You sure?" a girl wearing a South High Sprinters jersey asked. She was even shorter than me, but her legs looked about ten times stronger.

I nodded. "Thanks, though."

"I'll just make sure you're okay. I'll ride beside you for a little while," she said.

"You don't have to—"

"It's no big deal. I want to," she said. "We're all going to the same place, right?"

"I guess so," I said. Then I swung my leg over the bike, settled into the saddle, and started all over again.

CHAPTER 3

That afternoon we finished at a high school near Belfast, Maine, riding through an arch of red and white balloons. I might have been one of the last to finish, but I definitely wasn't absolutely last. I made sure of that.

"That counts, right?" I asked when I checked in.

"What are you talking about? Of course it counts," said the volunteer who was helping me. "You did great!"

As I was setting my bike in the right corral for the night, Cameron appeared beside me. "See? It wasn't that bad, was it?" he asked. "It's not brain surgery. You ride, you get tired, you rest, you ride again. The only thing you actually have to fear is boredom. The way the road starts to look when it's really hot and the pavement starts to shimmer."

"That didn't happen—yet." I didn't point out the wound on my elbow, or the fact that I had two Band-Aids on my hand. I'd thought it was too pretentious for me to wear gloves, but since my wipeout I'd put them on, just as Mason had suggested I do from the beginning. "Actually, it wasn't that bad, except for the part when I bit it."

"What happened there?" he asked.

"I spent some quality time on the pavement. Hit a pothole. No big deal."

"Yeah?" Cameron examined my elbow. "You want to go to the medical tent and make sure?"

"It's just scraped up. I'll put some ointment and a Band-Aid on it if it bugs me," I said.

"You know what this means," said Cameron.

"I'm clumsy?" I asked.

"No! It means you're officially a cyclist now. You have road burn."

"Oh joy," I said. "When do I get my member card or badge or whatever?"

Cameron pointed to my scraped forearm and elbow. "You're looking at it."

"Thanks," I said. "No, really."

The field was covered in a sea of blue tents. I found ours and located my duffel bag. Taking out my cosmetics bag and a change of clothes, I headed into the high school to find the locker room. I waited in line for a bit and then got to take a quick, hot shower. I didn't realize how much sweat and dirt there was on me until I washed it off. I felt like a new person when I was done.

After I got dressed and walked out of the little shower stall, I saw Autumn at one mirror, doing her hair, and Margo at another, putting on mascara. It was really weird to be hanging out with people I'd never spent time with at school. Not that we were "hanging out," exactly. We were just in the same real estate.

It was bizarre to see my blond hair in the mirror. I tried to run a comb through it, but didn't have much luck. The two-in-one shampoo my mom had bought because it would take up less room in my bag didn't have much conditioner, and I thought I was probably breaking my hair more than I was making it look nice. How would she know, though? My hair is nothing like my mom's. Mine has tight curls and looping waves because of my mixed-race background, while hers is stick-straight; she's half Japanese and half Caucasian. My dad is half African-American and half French. Which means I am officially four things at once, and my hair has a mind of its own.

I worked on it for a while, trying to make it presentable.

I was pretty sure that the fact I'd bleached it wasn't helping. I didn't even know how to react to seeing myself as a blonde. Without Stella to bounce the concept off, it was like I had no way to judge if I looked better or worse.

"So. You finished?" Margo asked.

"Not yet," I said. "I have some moisturizer—"

"No, I meant . . . you finished the ride?"

"Of course," I said with a laugh.

"Don't be so surprised I asked. You told us you were worried about it," Margo said. "I didn't know if you'd make it on your own or need the sag wag."

Margo really knew how to deliver an underhanded dig. "I did okay," I said, leaning forward to put lotion under my eyes. "I wish I were faster, but I'm still pretty new at this."

"It takes months of training," said Autumn, brushing her hair out after a blow-dry. "Months."

Outside, the smell of barbecue wafted through the air, and I made my way over to the row of grills, a large dinner spread of burgers, hot dogs, and various other food. I glanced at my phone. Thirty minutes until dinner started. I wasn't sure I'd be able to wait that long.

I wandered over to the support area: there was a small first-aid tent next to a tent offering free fifteen-minute leg massages. I peeked inside, but both massage tables were taken by others. I'd come back for that.

I climbed up on the bleachers by the football field, looking at over a hundred tents, all the same blue. The tents looked like a temporary camping convention, like base camp at Everest, but with more oxygen.

I fiddled with my phone. I really wanted to call Stella and tell her about this scene, but of course she already knew about it. She'd done this ride. She also knew how difficult Margo could be. She didn't need to hear that I was having a hard time with her.

I read through Stella's F-It List again. I had to get started.

That night we all gathered on the school's football field, sitting in the bleachers to listen to a couple of short, inspiring speeches by local kids who were cancer survivors, followed by a bluegrass band performing on a small stage on the edge of the field, facing us.

I looked at my phone, wondering when the official stuff would be over and when I could get started. I can't stand bluegrass and I definitely couldn't dance to it, which wouldn't make this semi-spontaneous dance party any easier.

"Have someplace else to be?" Cameron asked me.

"What?"

"You keep checking your phone. You have a date or something?" he asked.

I nearly snorted out the Gatorade I'd been drinking. "No. Definitely not. But I have something planned."

"Oh. Like, a Skype visit? FaceTime?" he said.

"Like that," I said.

The list was Stella's to share, not mine, and she wasn't ready, so I'd just have to appear spontaneously . . . weird. I wondered if I could present it as a "dare"-type scenario? That could make sense. Although Margo and Alex and Autumn would call me immature, they were probably going to call me that anyway.

At the moment Alex and Autumn were cuddling by the closed concession stand at the edge of the football field. I was starting to wonder if they'd only come on the trip so they could be together. Like, *together* together. Because there had been chunks of time when they'd been nowhere in sight. And cycling still didn't seem like their thing, but who was I to talk?

Margo was busy going over the next day's route on her phone, taking notes and crunching numbers. She had a spreadsheet spread out on the bleacher seat below us, and she was filling in information with a mechanical pencil.

"How are you feeling?" Margo asked.

"Fine," I said.

"Your legs aren't sore?"

"Nope."

"Just wait until tomorrow," she said. "I scoped out the route, and it's a lot harder. A lot."

Why did she sound like she was looking forward to that? As if she wanted my legs to feel terrible. She couldn't have been more obvious that she was going to take pleasure in my pain.

"So I was thinking," I said. *Both feet on the edge of the diving board. Now jump.* "What this place needs is a good party."

"You party?" asked Max, nodding. "Cool. There's a guy you might want to talk to—name's Scully. He—"

"No. Not party like that," I said quickly. At least, not yet. I'd have to remember the name Scully for future reference. "Just like, you know, dancing. Letting off steam. Having fun."

There was a deathly silence.

"I was thinking of turning in early, actually," Cameron said.

"No, you—you can't," I said. I only had three guys to choose from, because if I asked Alex to dance, Autumn would probably knock me out with one punch. "Come on, guys. We have less than a week away from home, so let's make the most of it, you know?" While I was talking and explaining the plan to turn the stage and football field into one big dance floor, Elsa vanished. I guess it wasn't her kind of thing.

"Yeah, all right. I'll go with you, too, find some speakers," Max offered.

"Might as well," said Oxendale. "It's not like I can fall asleep before midnight. Ever since I got here I've been running on the wrong clock."

"Fine. I'll come," said Margo.

"Great," I said. Now it was bound to be a *whole* lot of fun.

"Are you trying to be our team captain or something? Did Stella ask you to do that since she's not here?" Margo asked as we headed down the bleachers to the field when the band wrapped up.

"No, don't be ridiculous. Like I could be the captain," I scoffed.

"Exactly. That would be insane. Besides, we don't have a captain. But I still say you're up to something."

"I'm not *up* to something," I said.

"Then why do you get so mad every time I ask you a question?" she said.

"I don't know, maybe because you don't usually talk to me at school because you think you're too cool to, and now you're in my face?" I said. "You act like you *want* me to fail."

"No, I don't." Margo stopped walking and looked a little bit worried. "And I'm not trying to be in your face."

"Fine. Okay," I said. "But you're still doing a pretty good job of it."

"You're just upset because you're doing something that's not your normal thing," said Margo. "I mean, obviously. You're outside your comfort zone."

Way outside was more like it, but I wouldn't tell her that. "I'm not in any zone. I'm doing this because I want to."

Nothing like a conversation with Margo to motivate me. I quickly checked with Heather to see if it was okay if we made a little noise for a while by using the speaker system. I had to promise to end things by nine thirty, which was only half an hour away, but it still gave me enough time to get this task accomplished. I hooked up the phone and my dance playlist kicked out of the speakers, starting with a Fitz and the Tantrums song Stella and I loved.

I waited during the first song. I waited for other people to start dancing. No one did. Out of over three hundred people here, absolutely nobody was dancing. I didn't know Will that well, so I decided to start with the person I did know at least a little bit. "Cameron?" I asked. "Do you want to dance?"

"No," he said.

"What do you mean, no?" I said. "You didn't even pretend

to think about it." I pushed his arm gently.

"Oh, uh." He shook his head. "I don't dance."

"It's a rule?" I asked.

He nodded. "Yep."

"Okay . . . no problem. I get it." So much for that strategy. He wasn't the kind of person who danced, just like that.

"Um, Max?" I turned toward him, but just as I did, he headed straight for a tall girl with long, curly black hair. "Never . . . mind," I sighed.

A couple of minutes later Max and the girl were standing close, completely wrapped up in each other's attention. Then they started dancing, so at least they were playing along.

With Elsa hibernating in the tent, Autumn and Alex stuck together like glue, Max on the make, and Cameron completely saying no, my choice was down to Oxendale. He was staring at me expectantly, like he was waiting for me to make a move.

"I don't even remember seeing you at the last school dance," Margo said.

"I was working, probably. I'm always working," I explained.

Margo gave me a puzzled look. She didn't know that about me. She didn't know that I was saving for my own car, saving for a drawing class at an art studio that summer, and saving for a prom dress. Of course, I wasn't going to prom now.

"So, would you like to dance?" I asked Will.

"I'd be delighted." His face broke into a goofy grin. He seemed shy at first, barely catching the rhythm as he stepped back and forth. But as soon as we moved out closer to the other dancers, he leaped into action, slamming against me, against other dancers, hip-checking the speakers, taking out a small child—

Okay, I made that last part up. But the thing about being six foot six and skinny was that his elbows and knees were weapons.

Don't look at him, I told myself. *Forget that he's wearing a Connie's Cycles bike jersey that has the worst logo ever designed, with a wheel inside a wheel inside a . . . God, it makes me nauseous to look at it while we're dancing. Stop looking at it.*

I glanced out at the crowded field instead and saw dozens of other people moving, bouncing, unable to help themselves from dancing to Daft Punk, while others stood off to the sides, watching and talking. I hoped this would make Stella happy as I took a quick selfie of me and Oxendale.

"I love this song! Don't stop!" he shouted in my ear, pulling me to the center of the stage.

The sacrifices I was making for this list. Two down, eight to go.

◆◆◆

Half an hour later, the four of us were in our tent, getting ready for so-called lights-out. I planned to check in with my mom and send a photo or two to Stella. Elsa was reading in the farthest corner from me, Margo was obsessively straightening her sleeping bag because it kept sliding too close to mine, and Autumn was sitting cross-legged on the sleeping bag beside mine, brushing her hair the one hundred times we're all supposed to—again.

"You have a boyfriend, right?" Autumn asked. "So why did you want to dance with Oxendale?"

"Who, me? I don't have a— No, I'm not seeing anyone," I said.

"What about you and Oscar?" asked Margo.

My face burned. Why did I feel like she knew the truth but was bringing it up just to make me feel bad? "We're not a couple. Oscar likes seeing as many different girls as he can at the same time. Got it?"

Elsa looked up from her e-reader. "That's rude," she commented.

"Especially when you find out about it from other people," I said.

Autumn chugged water from her bike bottle. "Most guys are complete dogs. I mean, if you want to know why I'm with

Alex, it's because he'd never, ever cheat. We made a pact. I even have a promise ring. I didn't wear it on this trip because I didn't want to lose it."

"Promising . . . what?" I asked her.

"Don't you even know what a promise ring is?" Autumn asked.

"A place where everyone sits in a circle and promises stuff? Sounds cultish," I joked.

Stella would have laughed. Stella would have taken my idea and run with it. If she were here, the conversation wouldn't be awkward, wouldn't be a stretch. I wouldn't be answering these awful, embarrassing questions or getting to know way more about Autumn and Alex's commitment than I ever wanted to.

But instead, three blank faces looked at me.

"Okay, I know what a promise ring is," I said. "Good for you. I guess."

"So getting back to tonight," Autumn pressed. "You and Oxendale. Or do you call him Will?"

"There's no 'me and Oxendale,'" I whispered harshly, knowing the guys' tent was close by. "Can we talk about someone else now?"

"Sure. What about Stella? How's she doing? Is she going to be able to come see the finish, at least?" asked Margo.

"I hope so," I said. "I mean, she plans on it. Her parents are being really protective, though. They're worried about infection and stuff."

"I bet mine would be, too," said Autumn. "When I took a bad fall off the uneven bars in a meet, they made me quit gymnastics. Just *quit*."

"What if Stella has to quit cycling?" Elsa asked in her soft, quiet voice.

"Why would she quit?" asked Margo.

"Her parents could make her, just like mine made me. I mean, it's not the safest sport in the world," Autumn added.

Nobody said anything for a minute. I had this harsh image of Stella's crumpled bike in my head. I picked up my water bottle, which was half-full. "Oh, wow. I'm out of water. Be right back."

I slipped out of the tent. I needed air, not water. I headed for the refill station, enjoying the feel of the cool night air on my skin. I couldn't sit there while people asked prying questions about Stella. I just couldn't do it anymore. I was sick of lying.

"Hey," Cameron said. He was filling up a large Nalgene bottle. "Everything all right?"

"Pretty much," I said. *Or maybe, not so much,* I thought.

"One day down, six to go," he said.

"I wish you hadn't put it like that."

"You know what? I'm not sure I actually *like* camping all that much."

"At least you don't have to share a tent with Margo," I said. "She's calculated how many feet and inches we each get for our stuff. If your sleeping bag crosses the line, you're in trouble."

"That's the thing about camping. When it gets dark," Cameron said, "you can't go anywhere or do anything. You're kind of imprisoned."

"What about the fresh air and the great outdoors?" I asked.

He raised an eyebrow.

"It's a thing people say." I laughed. "I don't know."

"I like electricity. I like my bed. I like going to the electric fridge, in the middle of the night, and then going back to my bed."

"One day down, six to go?" I offered.

"That's lousy advice," he said.

Fred, one of the ride organizers, walked up to us as we stood there, sipping water. "Hey, how are you guys doing? Time to turn in, okay?"

We started walking back toward the Sparrowsdale sign by our tents. "Why does our team name have to be the Mighty

Sparrows?" asked Cameron. "How redundant."

"Hey, I wasn't even involved," I said. "I would have gone with the Golden Eagles or the Fighting Ospreys."

"Let's do that in yearbook. We'll change the name."

"It'll never fly," I said.

He groaned. "Good night already."

I went back into the tent. "Took you long enough," Margo commented.

"There was a line," I said, and slipped into my sleeping bag. Beside me, Autumn was texting, and Elsa was still reading. Across from me, Margo had put a sleep mask on and her sleeping bag was pulled up to her ears.

This was weird. Like a sleepover I'd never, ever have.

Like the one we did back in fifth grade, when we all camped as part of our elementary school graduation celebration. It rained and we huddled in leaky tents for two days, worrying about lightning.

Same as then, I knew that I was never going to fall asleep. I'd listen to the black flies buzzing outside and the coughs and conversations from other tents.

I was going to lie here all night and worry. About the ride. About how and when I'd get a pierced belly button. About Stella.

CHAPTER 4

The next time someone said "gentle, rolling hills," I'd know what they meant.

Hills.

Big, steep, horrible hills.

Lots of them.

My thigh muscles were burning as I started the last climb before our lunch break on Monday. Halfway up, since I was barely even moving, I got off the bike and started walking up it. While I was walking, other riders went past me, most of them standing up, pumping their legs.

Then other people who were walking their bikes, like me, started to pass me.

I was going to die on this hill, apparently. We'd turned

away from the coast and headed inland, which was not a good thing. It felt hotter and it was definitely steeper and buggier.

"Almost there!" a volunteer at the top of the hill shouted. "Keep it going!"

Keep what going? I wanted to respond. *My straggling pace, or the sweat that's rolling down the center of my back, like a mountain stream in spring?*

Behind me I heard a car engine and glanced over my shoulder to make sure I was far enough over on the side of the road. When we were riding in large groups I never worried, but now that I was almost all by myself out here, I had to check.

It wasn't a car. Well, it was, but it had a sign on the front: Official Support Vehicle For CCCR.

The so-called sag wagon was following me. That could only mean one thing. I was the last rider out here. If I slowed down any more, they'd sweep me up and toss me into the Subaru, no questions asked.

That did it. I was *not* showing up for lunch in the sag wagon. If I did, I'd never hear the end of it from Margo—and probably everyone else on the team. They'd long since abandoned me and left me to do this morning's ride on my own. As much as it hurt to ride, I was going to finish on the bike.

I got back on and forced myself to pedal the last quarter

mile. When I rode up to the finish line, there wasn't a cheer, or an announcement, or anything. There was one woman sitting at a table with a checklist. "Frances Marlotte?" she asked as I climbed off my bike.

"That's me."

"Nice going." She smiled at me. "It's not always easy, but it's always important. Now go on over and get yourself some lunch."

My mouth was already watering as I walked toward the large pavilion, where there were large pans of barbecued chicken, roasted vegetables, fresh watermelon, and carrot sticks. Everything was a little ransacked, but there was still plenty for me.

I was filling my plate when Cameron jogged up. "Where've you been? I was worried about you."

"I wasn't really into the rolling hills concept," I said. "It's more like steep hills with steep drops and then more hills."

"Don't worry, not every day will be like this," said Cameron.

"Nah, just *most* of 'em," said the woman who was dishing out cornbread. "Take my advice, hon. Go slow, enjoy the views, and eat lots of cornbread." She put another piece on my plate.

"You've done this ride?" I asked her.

"Oh, sure," she said. "With my bike club." Then she burst out laughing. "What are you, crazy? I couldn't finish this ride if my life depended on it."

Was she trying to make me feel better, or worse? It was hard to tell. I walked over toward a circle of rocks to sit down. I was halfway there when my right leg tightened. Then it seized. It felt like someone was squeezing on my calf muscle, or like it was caught in some sort of cruel industrial machine. I wanted to scream, and I couldn't walk.

I crouched down on one knee, wincing in pain, and some of my lunch fell onto the ground.

"What's up?" asked Cameron, taking my arm and helping me sit down.

"Leg . . . cramp," I gasped.

"Try to stretch it out," he said. He took my plate and picked up the food from the ground, shaking off the pine needles and dirt. "Three-second rule. You can eat this in a moment. First, extend your toes, then pull them back."

I tried pushing my toes forward, but they seemed stuck. "It's not working." I grimaced.

"Lie on your stomach for a sec. I'll rub it," he said.

I wanted more than anything to just eat my lunch, but it was kind of hard to do anything with my leg seizing up. When Cameron touched my calf, I nearly exploded from the sharpness of the sensation. He gently pushed on the muscle, forcing it to relax.

"So I've been thinking about our team," he said. "It's kind of like a microcosm of school."

I was too busy gritting my teeth to say anything. Or ask exactly what a microcosm was. It wasn't a word I actually used all that often.

"So there's the jock, Alex," he said, "and the jock's girlfriend, Autumn, who's an overachiever. We have the foreign transfer student, my pal Oxo. There's Elsa, the silent type, marches to the beat of her own drummer. Margo, well, not sure what category she would go in, honor society I guess." While he was talking, Cameron just kept massaging my calf. "There's the stoner burner guy who's super laid-back except for the fact he constantly chases girls. And then there's me and you. What categories do we go in?"

"Um . . . that makes it sound like a game show answer. I'll take: Names beginning with *F*," I said. "I'm not into cliques. I like to be friends with people from all different groups, you know?"

"Yeah, me too. But if you *had* to pick one group, because we're filling out our microcosm checklist, which would it be?" asked Cameron.

"Artists?" I mumbled into the ground. "Yearbook nerds?

People who work a lot at bad jobs? Wait. Do you have a job?"

"Summers only. I work at Cumberland Farms, which is neither a farm nor in Cumberland. But I think if I *had* to choose a group, I'd say techies. Coders."

"Stella's into coding," I said. "She wants to build apps. I mean, she's working on one."

"Oh, yeah? What will it do?"

"Something linking biking and restaurants," I said. "It could come in handy on something like this. If we ever got to stop."

"No doubt." Cameron nodded. "So how's she doing?"

"She's getting better," I said. "But she has a ways to go, still." Keep it vague, I reminded myself. "She messed up her pelvis. Which is such an embarrassing word."

"An unfortunate word," Cameron agreed. "Nothing makes me madder than drivers who don't look out for people who are biking. Have you ever seen those ghost bikes? They have them in bigger cities. They put white painted bikes where someone got hit—I mean, killed—by a car. Pretty creepy, but it has a really big impact on people. Maybe we should put one out by the scene—you know?"

I sat up abruptly and turned to look at him. "She didn't die," I said.

He was still holding on to my calf a little, and I pulled

away. Suddenly I felt like he could see right through me, like he knew everything. I almost shivered.

Right at that moment Margo walked by. She stopped and gave us a withering glance, holding an empty cup. "What happened to you? You fell down on the way to eat?"

"I just got a cramp, that's all." I stretched my leg, flexing my foot a little. Cameron gave my calf one last rub.

"Really, like, get a room!" Autumn laughed as she and Alex walked past.

"Did she really just say that?" I asked Cameron. "Of all people? They haven't been separated for two seconds since we started this trip."

"They should get a tandem bike," Margo agreed, arching one eyebrow. "Then they'd never have to be apart." She walked off, and I found myself smiling at her comment. She could have a sense of humor when she wanted to. As long as it wasn't about me, it was funny.

"Ooh, brownies—I'll grab us some." Cameron jumped up and walked over to the pavilion.

If I could have moved, I would have followed him. Instead, I ate my lunch quickly so I could check in with Stella. I'd told her I would call from the road on Monday.

"Hey! How are you doing?" I asked when she answered.

She kind of laughed, which was nice to hear. "I saw you

Saturday night. It's only been two days. I'm the same," she said.

"The exact same?" I asked. "Or kind of better or . . ."

"The same. What do you think? You think I'm going to jump out of bed and start running or something?" she snapped.

I didn't know exactly what I'd said to spoil her good mood. It had been happening a lot lately. I couldn't seem to say anything right anymore. "I didn't mean to imply anything," I said, trying to be patient. "I was just asking. I know—"

"You *don't* know, actually."

How could she say that to me? I was her closest friend. I'd done everything I could to understand what she was going through. I'd given her all the time and devotion I could, and I'd keep doing that forever. I was here for her, but she couldn't acknowledge it.

I stretched my legs, and immediately my calf started cramping again. I pressed my lips together, trying not to cry. The physical pain of my leg, plus the cold anger coming from Stella, was making my head spin.

"Frances?" she asked when I didn't say anything for a minute. "Are you still there?"

"I'm here," I said. *Are you?* I wanted to add. *Because it sure doesn't sound like you.* I was killing time, waiting for her to feel better. Whatever she wanted to take out on me, I had to accept. But our friendship wasn't the same, and I didn't know when it would be again.

When I got off the phone a minute later, Margo was standing beside me, staring at me, looking as critically at me as she always did. "What now?" I asked. "Am I late or something?"

"No." She shook her head. "I was just wondering something. How did you and Stella get to be friends? It's weird, because you're so different. She's such an amazing athlete and she's on the debate team and . . ."

And what? I'm nothing? I wanted to say. "You don't have to be the exact same as your friends. You know that, right?"

"I know. I know that," she said, sounding defensive.

"I'm friends with Stella because she's kind, and accepting, and she is more fun than anyone else I know," I said. "Being different . . . believe it or not? Some people think being different is actually a good thing."

She frowned at me. "You're not *that* different. You give yourself too much credit," she said.

"Whatever. You want to know how we became such good friends? I took a risk."

Sure, I was only nine at the time.

But my parents were in the middle of getting divorced,

and neither one of them had a lot of time for me. I had a couple of good friends, but not exactly a "best" friend, and when they were busy with ballet or piano—my parents didn't believe in spending money on lessons—I'd hang out by the baseball field that I passed on my way home from school.

There was this girls' softball team, fast pitch, ten and under.

I didn't know anything about softball, not really, other than when my dad pitched a ball, I could hit it. I was a good hitter, though I had no idea why—probably something genetic, because it wasn't like I worked on it all that much. It was just something my dad and I did.

About my fifth afternoon walking by, I stopped and asked the coach if I could be on the team. "We have a hole at second," she said. "Can you play second?"

Stella was the shortstop, and she quickly realized I didn't know much about the actual game, like rules, and she spent the first few days coaching me. I don't know to this day whether it helped when I joined the team or not. Stella was probably covering second and shortstop just fine on her own that day. But she never acted like I was hurting the team, and we had so much fun that spring that we'd been friends ever since.

Softball. It was something else she might not be able to do for a while.

"You don't strike me as a risk taker," Margo said.

"I'm here, aren't I?" I said.

"Yes, but you're only doing this out of guilt. That doesn't count."

"You don't know what you're talking about," I said. "I signed up for this long before Stella's accident. Stella and I are friends for a hundred reasons, but maybe mostly because we understand and support each other." *Something you've never tried to do,* I almost added.

Before we left for the afternoon's ride, I found Max making some adjustments to his bike. "Hey, uh, Max. You know that guy Scully you mentioned? Do you know what he looks like?" I asked.

Max looked up at me and then stood. "All right, all right. Now things are getting interesting."

"No, it's not, um, like that," I said.

"Sure it isn't." He smiled.

"Stella wanted me to say hi for her. Since you mentioned him, I thought maybe you could point him out to me?"

"Sure, come on," Max said. "I saw him grabbing some energy bars a minute ago when I was over there. His first name's Earl or Stanley or something. That's why he goes by Scully," he explained.

I followed Max over to the table labeled Provisions, where various sponsors had donated snacks to help us. I would not be taking any protein cubes. I was stuffed from lunch, besides.

A tall, broad-shouldered guy who looked more like a football player than a cyclist was standing in a group of people wearing matching Salisbury High jerseys. Max wasn't shy. He barged right in and pulled Scully aside.

"Scully, this is Frances. She's good friends with Stella. Who for some reason told her to look you up . . ."

"Your reputation precedes you, is what he's trying to say," I told him.

"Stella?" he asked.

"Dark-brown hair, about five-ten, long legs, wears black a lot, and rides a super-expensive silver bike—some Italian brand I can never remember."

"Stella, the speed demon. Hey, where is she? She around?" Scully asked.

"She couldn't come. She got into an accident, broke her leg," I explained.

"No shit. That sucks. Whoa." Scully rubbed the back of his neck. "Yeah, so, tell her I said hi. So you're riding for Sparrowsdale?"

I nodded and turned to Max for help, but of course he was chatting with another girl. "I was wondering if . . . you know. . . there's any way you might know of somebody who might . . . possibly . . . have something to drink?"

He grinned. "I'll be hosting a little event tonight. Drop by around eight."

CHAPTER 5

It was late afternoon when I finally arrived in Bath, crossing the huge bridge over the Kennebec River.

Funny. If there was one thing I really needed, it was a bath.

There were no words for how my muscles felt as Cameron and I drifted across the finish line. What muscles, actually? Maybe that was the problem. The small amount I'd built up over the past few weeks had been pummeled to smithereens.

I'd always wondered about the word "smithereens." Now I knew the right use for it.

As I finished setting my bike in our group's section of the big open field on Monday—we were staying at a campground that night—I nearly staggered after Cameron, following him to the truck where we could fetch our gear. I needed a shower. I needed new clothes.

Cameron had kept pace with me the whole afternoon. He'd cheered me on. He'd laughed when I complained. He'd pointed out all the scenery, quite the tour guide, while I ground out the miles. Yes, Maine was pretty. Yes, the ocean view, when we saw it, was breathtaking. No, I didn't ever want to see any of it again if it reminded me of how I felt right now. I'd move to the opposite coast, or somewhere way, way inland, like Ohio or something.

Then again, maybe not. Whenever we turned inland everything got a little more hilly.

But having him beside me had made a big difference. I'm not sure I would have finished if he hadn't helped me. I was still at the back of the pack, but it didn't matter that much. Until now, when I realized that even walking was painful. It was like my legs were so conditioned to riding a bike that they'd forgotten how to work without one.

Cameron was being so nice—riding with me, giving me a leg massage, making sure I got enough to eat. If other members of the team didn't like me because I was a much slower version of Stella, then at least Cameron was on my side.

It almost made me wonder if Stella had hired him to take

care of me. Or maybe my mom had slipped him a few twenties and asked him to look out for me.

Of course, one other option was that he was actually interested in me.

Since the leg massage, I'd found myself wondering if maybe *I* was interested in *him*.

It was the kind of thing I'd want to talk over with Stella, if she were here. We usually overanalyzed anything involving crushes and boys—or at least, I did. When I was wavering about breaking up with Oscar, Stella got so sick of listening to me that she nearly broke up with him *for* me.

Cameron was nothing like Oscar; there wasn't anything about him that screamed sleazeball or even cheeseball. He was kind, slightly goofy, a slouchster but a good athlete who didn't act conceited.

But I was here on a mission, and it wasn't to hook up with someone on the team; even if I did need to have an epic kiss, I'd try to have it with someone not from Sparrowsdale. Having one more romance on our team would make everything incredibly awkward—or *more* awkward. I could keep getting to know Cameron better without putting a label on it for the next little while. For all I knew, he had a girlfriend. That was the weird thing about this trip with a bunch of relative strangers; our lives at school hardly intersected, but suddenly here we were, relying on one another.

I grabbed my duffel, Cameron got his, and we headed for the campground showers. We separated at the locker room entrances.

Naturally, Margo was walking out of the locker room just as I was walking in; she'd probably been done for hours. She was wearing a short-sleeved tee, shorts, and flip-flops, her long, dirty-blond hair was swept into a braid, and she had full makeup on, with her cosmetics bag hanging from her wrist. I didn't spot a single drop of sweat on her. She smelled like perfume and hair spray. I, on the other hand: indescribably rank.

I tried to walk past her with a brief nod, but she stopped in front of me. "You're not looking so good."

"Thanks so much," I said. "That's always nice to hear."

"Are you okay?" she pressed. "You're limping."

"A little sore, that's all."

"Hold on a second, I have something." She unzipped her cosmetic bag and pulled out an unmarked orange prescription bottle. She shook a couple of red pills into her palm and held them toward me. "Here, have these. They'll make you feel better."

"Um . . ." I studied the bottle as well as I could.

"Relax. It's ibuprofen. What did you think, that I was going to give you something prescription or illegal?" She acted as if this was the first time anyone had ever doubted her. About anything.

"Well, you have to admit. 'Have these, you'll feel better' is the phrase they warned us about in seventh-grade health class. Plus, you could be pulling a Lance Armstrong–type thing," I said.

She pressed the ibuprofen tablets into my palm. "Take these or don't take them. You are an idiot." She zipped up her little bag and sashayed away, leaving me with two melting pale-red pills in my hand. They looked like budget M&M's, the color nobody wanted that failed.

I went to the drinking fountain and washed them down with a couple of sips of freezing-cold water. If she was trying to poison me, I wasn't sure I cared at that exact moment. And if it was something to give me a competitive edge, wasn't that exactly what I needed?

"All right, Franny!" Oxendale clapped me on the back just as I stood up, causing me to nearly knock my teeth into the faucet. "You made it."

I turned around and looked up at him. He was wearing a fresh cycling jersey; he'd explained his system of wearing a new one the night before to get him psyched for the next day. He'd gone on and on over breakfast about his theory of packing light, but I'd been too sleepy to care.

I brushed the water off my mouth with the back of my hand. "I'm here," I said to Oxendale. "For better or worse."

"I see." He nodded. "Well done, mate. It's going to get easier from here on out. Trust me."

Somehow, I didn't.

"Well. Maybe not technically easier. I could be wrong about that," he admitted. "Say. If you talk to Stella later, tell her I said hello, would you?"

"Sure, no problem." That was, if she would talk to me. I wandered into the locker room, which was emptying out. All that much easier to find a vacant shower stall, where I could collapse in private. The layers of dirt and sweat on my legs dissolved while I stood in the hot water with my face to the showerhead, enjoying every drop.

"So what's the deal?" Max asked as we headed across the field of tents that evening.

I couldn't believe I was actually about to do the most daring item on the list yet.

I'd had to be subtle about asking Max to come with me. I didn't want Margo asking where we were going. I didn't want to invite anyone else and risk getting them into trouble. I didn't have that worry about Max; he was used to handling himself in this kind of situation. In fact, I was trusting him to help me smoothly carry out this list item.

"What do you mean?" I asked him. "There's no deal."

"You're not . . . I've never seen you at house parties or behind school or anything," Max said. "You seem pretty straight and narrow."

"You just don't know me," I bluffed. "Anyway, we're away from home. I want to have fun. I told Stella I'd live adventurously for her."

Max laughed. "I'm not sure if that counts as an excuse."

"Fine," I said. "Then what's yours?"

"I'm not . . . I don't . . . listen, don't tell anyone. But I'm not a big partier. At all. I just hang out with some."

Before I could even react, we'd reached the Salisbury tent banner. I couldn't follow up with a question like, *Are you serious? How dumb do you think I am?*

"Scully?" Max asked. "Which tent are you in, man?"

"Who goes there?" a deep voice replied.

"Dude, it's Max and Frances."

The tent unzipped and a tall guy with shoulder-length blond hair peeked out. I didn't recognize him without his helmet. "Hey. What's up? How's it going?"

If I were to be honest, I'd say that I felt like one giant mass of pain. But nobody would want to hear that. "Not bad," I said. "How are you guys?"

"Come on in," he said, holding open the tent door for us. "Make room, make room. Incoming."

Max and I ducked into the tent, which was exactly like mine, except that seven people were inside of it now instead of four, making it a tight fit. The screens were open to let the breeze through, and I found a spot sitting between Scully and a girl I recognized from the first day.

Scully made some quick introductions, then said, "As all of these Scullywags already know, we're running low tonight, so we'll have to share."

Scullywags? Okay. It might be the strangest name for a group I had ever joined, stranger even than being on the Sparks dance team. "Right, okay," I said with a shrug, like it was something I did all the time.

He shook a bike bottle like he was making a concoction in chemistry class. Then he squirted some into his mouth and handed the bottle to me. "Pass to the left," he said.

"What, uh, what is this?" I asked.

"Spiked lemonade," Scully said. "Think of it as Gatorade with a kick. A big kick."

I braced myself. I knew it wasn't going to taste good.

This was a big deal for me. Once upon a time, Stella and I had pledged not to drink in high school. We'd sworn to have as much fun as we could without breaking any laws. We both needed scholarships for college. Grade point averages and clean records were important to us. Or maybe they *had* been, until Stella shared her list with me and I learned she wanted to do things differently, on this trip at least.

So here I was, throwing caution to the wind thanks to Stella's list. If she could see me now, hanging out with this crowd . . . she'd laugh. Not that she was talking to me, or laughing, because she wasn't. But someday, she would see or hear about this and it would make her happy. I hoped.

"Cheers? Is that a thing?" I laughed nervously. Then I opened wide and squirted a stream down my throat.

The sourness of it combined with whatever had spiked it made me instantly pucker my lips. I'd gulped way too much. I passed the bottle to my left.

Scully leaned over to me, his longish blond hair brushing my arm. "What you do is, you pack one bottle already filled with something. Then all you need to find is a mixer," he said.

Great. Now Scully was taking me under his wing as, like, someone who needed to be educated in the ways of trouble-making. Which was kind of true. I didn't veer off the beaten path very often.

"What team are you on again?" he asked.

"Max's team. From Sparrowsdale," I said. "Little town in northern New Hampshire?"

"Right, right." He looked at Max, who was in the middle of a very intense conversation on the other side of the tent with a girl with spiky black hair and a neck tattoo. "You're not, like, with him, are you?"

"Oh, no." I shook my head. "Not even . . . close."

"Good. Love the guy as a friend, but he takes the word 'player' to a whole new level. I am not here to hook up, if you know what I mean."

"Oh, I do. I do." I nodded. "I'm way too busy trying to survive."

He laughed. "No, for real."

"For real," I said.

"Maybe this will help." He guzzled another gulp of lemonade. "You know, you—we—we are all doing an amazing thing here. We deserve to kick back and unwind. This is nothing. Wait until we hit Phantom Park." He handed me the bike bottle, which was nearly empty.

I didn't want to think about what would happen then. I took another drink and then handed it back to him. "I think this is empty?"

"Time for a new batch." He got out two more bike bottles,

did some mixing, and handed me a fresh batch. "Taste this for me, would you?"

Like I would know what it was supposed to taste like, I squirted some into my mouth. It tasted more bitter than the last one, which probably meant it had more alcohol in it. "It's a bit strong," I said as I handed it to the girl on my left. This was a weird ritual.

"So back to Phantom Park," Scully said. "I'm making plans with some friends to meet us there. Reinforce our supplies."

"Are we going into battle or something?" I laughed. I could feel the drink starting to affect me, which meant I should probably slow down.

Phantom Park was a huge New England attraction. A man who made his fortune in baked beans or something ridiculous like that built this giant English castle for his family on a huge estate. When he went bankrupt, the castle was rumored to be haunted. Finally, some company bought the land and turned it into a massive amusement park—complete with a haunted house.

"There are still rooms in that abandoned mansion that no one has ever gone into. But we—we will," Scully said, and the girl beside me nodded in agreement.

"It'll be epic," she said.

"Is that going to be a problem—I mean, won't we get in trouble?" I asked.

"You. Need to live a little." He handed me the bike bottle, which seemed to have made its last circuit in record time. "Your turn."

Max's eyes met mine across the circle, and he lifted a bottled water in my direction.

I never would have guessed that Max wasn't a partier at all.

Or that I, apparently, was.

CHAPTER 6

I left the party after a little while, but I didn't want to head back to my tent. I wanted to stay outside in the fresh air until it got dark, until I had to go back into the land of the weird sleepover.

I was pretty sure we'd be sent packing if we were caught drinking. Besides, I was worried that in trying to do good, I was setting a bad precedent. Just because Stella put it on the list as a whacked-out, crazy thing to do, that didn't mean I had to see it through.

But I knew I wasn't doing anything super impressive by bailing early on the night. Besides, I had a feeling I was already a little too swamped and tipsy. When I walked, I didn't always go in a straight line.

There was really only one person I wanted to talk to right now.

I stopped on my way back to the tent and found a private place to sit, under a tree on the outskirts of the tent area.

"Hey. Are you up?"

"Of course I'm up," Mason said. "It's only nine thirty."

"Oh, I thought it was later. Really? It's nine thirty?"

"You're probably tired because you rode all day. Makes it feel later," said Mason.

"Probably. Sure," I may have slurred.

"Are you okay?"

"Sure I'm okay."

"You sound weird."

"I'm fine."

"If you say so. How did it go today?"

"It was brutal. But I survived. How's Stella? Is everything okay? I called her at lunch and she was really . . . mean, actually."

"You know. She's, um . . . She had a setback today. The doctors wanted her to try some exercises in rehab, and it didn't go well. But she's fine."

I didn't say anything for a minute. She was anything but "fine," which Mason knew. There was no point bringing it up.

"Mason?" I said.

"Yeah."

"It's really *pretty* here."

"Uh-huh," he said.

"But when do you think Stella's going to *really* get better?"

"Nobody knows, for sure. But in a month or so—"

"Before summer?" I asked. "By next Saturday night? 'Cause we swore we'd go to prom together," I said.

"Prom isn't all it's cracked up to be," said Mason.

"I know," I said. "That's why I wanna go. To see how awful it is. But she's gotta go with me. I can't go if she doesn't. And I know it's not important at all, in the grand scheme of things, but it's important because we made these plans—no, *she* made these plans and—sometimes you really need to follow the plan."

"I think you should probably go to sleep now, Franny."

He was right. I was babbling. "I know. I have to go. Anyway, my battery's dying," I said. It had been beeping at me during our conversation, but I hadn't wanted it to end. "G'night."

I knew I wouldn't have time to charge my phone in the morning, so I got up from my secluded spot and headed for the charging station set up outside the campground rec center. It emitted a soft glow with the lights of phones, which was oddly comforting. I found a cord—thank goodness they had extra chargers, because I couldn't have found mine in the dark in the tent. Especially since I was a little woozy.

I stepped back from the long folding table and wondered if I could leave my phone here to charge while I went to bed. Probably not. Sure, my phone case was distinctive enough—a geometric black-and-white pattern that made you feel like it went on forever when you looked at it—but then again, look at this crowd. There were just too many phones here.

I sat on the ground and looked up at the stars, which seemed even brighter tonight than usual. I was gazing at the constellations when somebody nudged my ankle. "Mind if I . . ." Margo held up a phone cord.

"No, it's okay," I said, my eyes closing as I tried to wait up until my phone had more percentage points. Maybe it was already high enough right now, because I wasn't sure I wanted to sit beside Margo for the next hour.

"Do you want me to wait up for yours?" she suddenly asked. "I have to be here anyway."

That sounded so nice, I almost said yes. But this was Margo. "No thanks. I'm kind of enjoying being out here."

"Me too. The tents make me claustrophobic," she said. "If I could sleep out here instead, I'd do that, but I hate bug bites more than anything." She brushed her leg, whether at a mosquito or something else, I wasn't sure. "So. You going to tell me or what?"

"Tell you?"

"Why you did that dance thing last night."

"I just thought it would be fun," I said. "Stella told me that I should try to have a good time on this trip, and since riding isn't exactly always fun for me, then I have to create fun another way."

She looked as if she didn't believe me, as if she had something else on her mind. "Seems like a strange way to have fun. Did you only do it so you could send Stella a picture?"

"That was part of it," I said. "She's still really upset she couldn't be here."

"Is she going to sign up for something else? You know, like, maybe this summer?"

Her question caught me completely off guard. "What do you mean?"

"Another ride," she said. "There's one in July—how long does it take a broken leg to heal? I can't remember."

"I don't know if she'll be ready for that," I said. "But when she is—yeah, I'm sure she will."

There was an awkward silence between us that went on for so long that I was about to bail, charge or no charge, when Margo said, "I know. Okay?"

"Know what?" I replied.

"About Stella," she said. "What's really going on."

She doesn't know anything, I told myself. *She's bluffing, looking for information.* If she could pretend, then I could, too. Margo was the last person in the world I'd want to tell something secret to.

"She might say she's okay, but she's not okay. I tried to FaceTime with her once she was back home—she only talked to me for a couple of minutes, but I saw how she looked. Her face. It's the same look my mom has," Margo said.

I took my time responding. I didn't want her to think I was too eager to know her theories. "What look is that, exactly?" I asked.

"Like she's totally unhealthy and miserable. Like there's something big wrong, something she's not telling us," said Margo. "And you're keeping it a secret, too."

"No. There isn't," I said. "Margo, she got hit by a car. How do you expect her to look and feel?" She didn't say anything. "What's going on with your mom?"

"She has colon cancer and she's doing chemo," said Margo. "One week on, one week off. It's her second time through it. The last time wasn't totally successful."

I felt awful, thinking of Margo's mom, who used to be one of my mom's closest friends. That was how Margo and I ended up at the same preschool. The fact that we didn't get along made it hard for my mom to schedule playdates for the four of us—even back then.

Why hadn't I known about this? Did my mom know about it? "Whoa. Margo, I had no idea. Why didn't you tell us?"

"What am I going to say? Hey, everyone, my mom is pretty ill, actually. Yeah, so. Have a great day."

I couldn't respond. She had a point. "That's too bad. I'm sorry."

"Yeah, well. Not much anyone can do. Just treat it, you know? Meanwhile, she's wasting away to nothing. Have you seen my mom lately? She's a rail," Margo said bitterly.

I pictured Stella, who'd barely been eating. Lately, her meals consisted of high-protein shakes that I'd never seen her actually finish.

I couldn't believe Margo was confiding in me like this. She never talked to me on this level. I was tempted to tell her about Stella. If she was willing to be this vulnerable, then maybe I should be, too. I could at least be honest with her.

But it wasn't what I wanted to do that mattered; it was what Stella wanted and needed. I'd sworn to keep her condition a secret.

"I'm so sorry to hear that," I said. "How long will it last? I mean, the chemo? How long will it be until she starts feeling better?"

I didn't ask her what I really wanted to know. The questions I had been asking myself every day since I'd agreed to participate in the race. Like: *How can you be out here, riding, when she's at home? How do you deal with worrying about her in the middle of the night? How can you think about time trials and winning?*

"Who knows?" said Margo. "She stops this round in a week, and after that, I guess . . . I don't know."

I wanted to offer her a hug, even though that wasn't my style. She looked so miserable. But this was the same person who'd ignored me for the past four years. On the other hand, did it make sense to hold a grudge at this point?

It's just a hug. It's not like you're signing a NATO peace treaty.

I ended up compromising by giving her a super-awkward pat on the arm, which probably just made Margo uncomfortable.

"You're drunk, aren't you?" she suddenly asked.

"What?"

"You smell like a disgusting bar. Why am I even bothering with you?"

"I'm not drunk," I said. "I don't know what you're talking about."

"You are. Go brush your teeth. You are *not* getting us kicked off this trip."

"Fine. Listen, if you talk to your mom, tell her I said hi." I unplugged my phone, thinking that was probably the stupidest thing I could have said just then.

I stopped halfway to the tent and looked back at Margo. She was leaning against a picnic table bench, crouched over her phone, a soft glow lighting her face while she typed intently.

Everyone had secrets. Everyone. It was just that I'd promised Stella to keep hers.

CHAPTER 7

"Come on, Franny, get up. Rise and shine!"

I groaned at the sound of Oxendale's overly energetic voice. "I can't get up. And quit calling me Franny," I mumbled into my pillow on Tuesday morning. Only Stella was allowed to call me that—and her family, by extension.

I slowly opened my eyes to see Oxendale and Cameron standing in the tent's doorway. Oh, crap. If Cameron was up, then I was definitely late.

"You're going to miss breakfast," Cameron said.

I sat up and looked around the tent, quickly realizing that not only were all the other girls up, but they'd already packed. The place was bare.

Then it came back to me: the night before . . .

Chugging vodka lemonade or whatever it was with Scully and the "Scullywags."

Calling Mason and babbling.

The heart-to-heart with Margo.

I wanted to lie back down, slide into my sleeping bag, and hide.

"Where is everyone?" I asked, rubbing my cheeks with my fingers, trying to snap out of the dream I was having that I already couldn't remember.

"Late night?" asked Cameron.

"No," I said. "Well, maybe."

"Max told us you were fraternizing with some other teams," Oxendale commented. "Said you left early and he had no idea where you went."

Fraternizing? What did that even mean? "That's because he's Max and he took off with some new girl," I said. "He had no idea that I came back here."

"What's your story then?" asked Cameron.

"There's no story. I came back here and I, uh, crashed." My head was pounding, I was already tired, but it was time to get up and start this whole thing over again. I climbed out of the tent, crouched over, and nearly screamed in pain.

It was my legs—more specifically my calves, and my

quads, and come to think of it, my back, and my ankles weren't so good, either.

Cameron grabbed me by the arm to keep me from falling. "Muscle cramp again?"

"Is that what you call it? It feels like muscle death."

"You need another massage," Cameron said, and I wasn't sure if he meant a professional effort or one of his own, like the rubdown he'd given my ankles and calves the day before. I blushed, thinking about his hands on my legs. "But in the meantime, walk around and they'll stretch out."

"You mean, limp around? I can do that." I winced with every step as I headed to the breakfast buffet, taking short, mincing steps, like an older person might. Three lonely bagels remained on a serving tray, along with some slightly cold scrambled eggs and an orange. I don't even like oranges, but I couldn't afford to be picky.

I gulped some juice and water, ate quickly, then hurried to get changed and ready for the start of the day's ride. I made sure I had everything I needed for the day, then stashed my duffel, sleeping bag, and sleeping pad at the truck, in the spot reserved for our team.

I stopped for a minute to read the "Current Standings" list posted on the inside of the truck. Instead of times, the list tracked money raised. Thanks to our fast riders, we'd earned two thousand dollars extra so far. Lucky for me, or for the cause, actually, dollars were not deducted based on my finishing times.

I heard a horn blare five times in the distance—that meant five minutes until starting time.

I ran over to my bike and quickly grabbed my water bottles, filled them, and placed them in their metal holders. Then I headed to the starting line and got ready to shove off with everyone else.

While Heather's daily instructions and inspiring remarks drifted over the crowd, I looked around, trying to figure out where the rest of my team was. I started at the front and walked toward the back. Margo was at the front—no surprise there. A few rows back were Oxendale and Cameron, and off to the side were Alex and Autumn in matching colors, head to toe, enough to make me puke even if I hadn't also just downed a bagel and orange in four minutes flat.

I spotted Max—his tattooed arms made him stand out in a high school crowd—beside the same girl he'd vanished with the night before. I got into line at the back. There was a nudge against my back tire, and I turned to see Elsa pushing her way up beside me. "You and me," she said. "We'll ride."

"You'll ride with me?" I asked, incredulous. Elsa might be quiet, but she was amazingly fast. Stella told me that Elsa had once won a time trial but refused to take the medal because she felt it should go to someone else for courage. So she was a bit of a space cadet, but also extremely sweet, and skilled. It was a combination I wasn't used to. How could she be so fast and so numbers-oriented on the bike and yet never turn in homework on time, or even keep track of her class schedule? I could think of endless times she'd drifted into a class, late, or I'd see her out in the school courtyard with her headphones on, when she was supposed to be in French with me.

"Sure, of course," she said. She always talks in this dreamy voice, even though she barely ever says more than one sentence. It was like she was reciting poetry, a few careful words at a time. You started to feel lucky she was talking to you, that you got her precious wisdom. But then she'd say something completely screwball.

The horn blew, and when I pushed off, my legs felt like lead. I was moving at a turtle's pace, or it felt that way, anyway. I'd have liked to see a turtle—even a slug—ride as slowly as I did at the start, my bike weaving a little like a deflating balloon that's going down, down, down. . . .

Stay on the bike, I told myself. *It's for Stella. You can't start the day by falling.* I gradually steadied myself and the bike and got a grip, literally and figuratively.

"Flat course," Elsa said after a bit, when the road leveled out.

"I'm going slow," I told her. "The whole way."

A few minutes later she added, "No worries," in her wispy voice.

I glanced over at her as we reached a good cruising speed a bit later, when we got onto a different road where the shoulder was wide enough to ride side by side. As long as I didn't push myself too hard, I could do this for a while. Then I saw a steady stream of water sliding from Elsa's eyes to her ears, through her helmet's chin strap.

"Elsa?" I asked. "Are you crying?"

"No. Maybe a little," she said.

"Are you okay?"

She nodded. "Seasonal allergies," she said, the words rolling off her tongue like song lyrics, like seasonal allergies are something you wished you had.

I looked ahead at the long, flat section, and saw riders stretching out even more than yesterday, some attacking at the front and some relaxing. We were a long, winding chain that was loose but still connected. It was something I thought about re-creating somehow—in a drawing, maybe a painting.

Maybe I could become a cyclist after all, at some point, because it felt really cool, even if I was at the back. Now I knew what Stella was talking about—even if this might never have been *her* view, from way back here.

I reached for my phone to take a picture, so I'd have it to work from. Only it wasn't in the little handlebar bag where I'd been keeping it. I pulled off to the side of the road and started searching. It wasn't in my bike seat bag, not in my baggy shorts' side pockets, not in my zippered back pocket.

Elsa peeled around and came back to me. "What is it?" she asked.

"I can't find my phone. Can you call it for me?" I waited for her to take out her phone and then listed the digits. She dialed, and I waited. But there was no sound, nothing at all.

I'd lost my phone.

It had the past three years of photos on it. Photos of me and Stella. Three years of music downloads. Three years of memories. My entire high school existence.

"Where are you going?" asked Elsa as I got ready to head in the opposite direction.

"My phone—it has to be back at the tent site. I'll get back there before they pack up."

"You can't," Elsa said.

"I have to. The phone has everything!" I said. "I have to. Go ahead, it's okay. I'll find the sag wagon and have them take me."

"They can't," said Elsa.

Her soothing voice had no effect on me right now; in fact, just the opposite. "Go *ahead*, I'll catch *up*," I told her, and she looked at me uncertainly, head tilted, like a cat who didn't understand why I wasn't sharing that bowl of cereal with her. I knew the idea of me catching up to her or to this pack in general was ludicrous, but I didn't have an option.

I pushed off and started riding as hard as I could against the oncoming line, on the other side of the road. "Wrong way!" a few people yelled to me, as if this was amusing, and I just looked down at the road and kept pumping. I'd find the tent, I'd find my phone.

When the sag wagon saw me, the driver, Fred, signaled me to stop. "What's going on, Frances?" he asked.

"I lost my phone." I started babbling, telling them how it was invaluable, how it was almost a part of me.

"It's just a phone. And you can't go back," Heather told me. "We're fifteen miles out already."

"We are?" I really needed to start paying attention to the little counter on the handlebars. It had valuable information, apparently.

"Yes—"

"But that's only ten minutes by car," I said. "We can zip back and—"

Heather shook her head. "No, we can't."

"Can everyone stop saying *can't* for a second?" I cried.

"Look, there are things we can do, but we can't go back right now. While Fred drives, I'll call the grounds crew, the truck. We'll have them search the tent, your bag, and everything," Heather said. "Okay? Now, I'm going to need a description of the thing, so how about you ride with us for a while?"

"The miles—the ride. I have to get that done," I said, even as I climbed off the bike and watched Fred effortlessly put it in a bike rack on top of the Subaru.

"You'll get back on the road soon. We'll just get a good description of what you lost," Heather said. I slid into the backseat; Fred slid into the driver's seat and closed the door, and we were off. "You want to tell me what kind it is, what the case looks like?" Heather asked.

It felt so good to sit down in a car. I gave a long description of the phone, with all the details anyone would need to find it: black-and-white case, screen crack on the lower right, home screen a photo of Stella and me. I listened as she called in the report and waited for an answer. It was agonizing.

"No? Nothing like that?" Heather said finally. "Well, did you find her bag?" Again, the waiting. "Okay. Keep looking, would you? Thanks." She turned around and held up her hands. "Nothing yet. They're trying. Maybe later it'll surface."

I wasn't sure a phone had ever surfaced when I'd been looking for it, except for that one time when I was thirteen and I put my mom's in the washer by mistake and realized it fifteen minutes later. Then it surfaced. Like a dead white fish.

"So, how's the ride going for you?" Fred asked. "Day three, how are we feeling?"

"We're feeling like . . ." *Crying, actually.* "Okay, I guess. Pretty sore. It's the first time I've done it, so . . ."

"How'd you get involved?" Heather asked. "I mean, was there a specific reason, a person you're doing it for?"

"My best friend did it last year. She convinced me to do it, too. She was the one spearheading the whole thing for our team. Then she, uh, got hit by a car," I explained. It sounded so dramatic and tragic when I said it. Probably because it *was*. We were too young to be having near-death experiences. "Stella Grant?"

"Oh, man, that was a shame. She was so looking forward to coming back. A great fund-raiser—I think she won the girls' daily challenge three days in a row last year, wasn't that right?" Heather asked.

"At least three. I think it was actually four times," said Fred.

"She never mentioned that," I said. "Four times in a row?" That was so like her, to do something extreme and just not tell anyone. Her dad had some mantra he was always telling her and her brothers, "The pride is in doing it, not talking about it."

Me? I'd take out TV ads if I ever did something so amazing.

Heather's phone rang and I crossed my fingers, but it wasn't good news about my phone. It was details about lunch. Just hearing Heather talk made me feel slightly hungry.

"So how is Stella doing? Is she healing okay?" Heather asked me when she finished the call.

"Um, yes." I nodded. "She's sort of . . . she's fine, actually."

"Hopefully she'll be able to do the ride next year," Fred said, "and you two can come back together."

I tried to smile but couldn't quite pull it off. There were so many things that had to happen before then.

I bit my lip to keep from choking up while the Subaru buzzed past several riders, and I scanned them to see anyone from Sparrowsdale, but we were traveling too fast. We pulled into a small parking lot on the side of the road, outside a restaurant. "Okay if we let you out here?" Fred asked.

"Um, sure." I got out of the car and brushed my eyes with the back of my leather glove while Fred got my bike down for me. He checked the air in the tires, added a little, then returned it with a smile. "See you at the road's end!"

I tried to smile back, but I was feeling pretty bad. Not only did I have a small hangover, I guess, but my will was pretty much gone. Still, I adjusted my helmet, reset my computer, and carefully made my way back into the pack of riders.

Margo suddenly appeared at my side, pedaling beside me. "That's cheating, you know."

I switched to a higher gear, pedaled harder. "You can keep on riding, you know."

"Are you injured?" she asked. "Because you're riding like you're not."

"I'm not. I lost my phone, so I tried to get them to go back and help me find it, but they wouldn't," I explained. *Not that I need to explain myself to you.*

"Seriously? Crap," Margo cursed. "What are you going to do?"

"I don't know," I said. "I really don't." I reached for my water bottle and took a few gulps. We rode together for a few minutes. It actually didn't feel bad to be side by side. If everyone on this team supported me like this, I knew I'd be able to finish out the week, even if I hobbled in to the finish.

Margo cleared her throat. "I was hanging back, wondering where you were," she said. "But now I know you're okay, so—I'm going ahead. I can't ride this slowly for long. Makes my legs all jumpy."

"You do what you have to do," I muttered, wishing I could bop her with my water bottle, but she was already out of reach. I'd drift to the back where I was comfortable, *maybe too comfortable,* I thought as I watched her speed up and start passing people.

Why didn't anyone ride this like an actual team? In the Tour de France, which Stella has made me watch every year for the past three years, the teams all bunch together to support their best rider.

Huh, maybe that's it. I'm not the best, and I can't keep up with the best, so I should probably stop comparing this to the Tour. This isn't a tour. This is a gut-wrenching, muscles-burning journey. On my own.

Stella wasn't here to save me, the way she usually did when things got too hard.

I started pedaling harder. As I pumped my legs, the bike weaved a little. I wobbled into the middle of the road.

"Hey, watch it!" a girl trying to pass me yelled. "On your left!"

"Sorry!" I called, correcting my line.

"Oh. It's okay," she said, riding beside me for a second. "I just don't want to bite it."

I nodded. "Neither do I."

We pedaled side by side.

"The good thing about riding in the back? Fewer people see your screwups." She laughed.

I smiled. Maybe I'd get that printed on one of those cute little motto signs they sold at gift shops.

Ride in the Back. No One Will See Your Screwups.

Ride in the Back. No One Will See You Crash.

Just . . . Ride in the Back.

CHAPTER 8

"We're kicking ass as a team, you know that?" Max said at lunch.

I'd gotten there later than most people, but this time lunch was sub sandwiches, and there were plenty left to choose from. I'd taken extra bags of potato chips to stash for later; the salt would taste good when I was near death.

My team was sitting in the shade, under a tree beside a huge, beautiful lake that I wanted to dive into in all my clothes. Everyone was talking about the morning, how Max, Oxendale, and Alex had been third, fifth, and seventh in a wild sprint finish. "It's all going according to plan," Cameron said confidently, leaning back against a tree trunk, straw in his mouth.

"You forgot your evil laugh," said Oxendale. "You can't talk like a supervillain without an evil laugh."

"When did I become a villain?" Cameron wondered out loud. He looked at me and raised his eyebrows. "Is this trip starting to take a turn into a weird area?"

"I've always thought it was in a weird area," I said.

"No, it's just we're back in New Hampshire," said Oxendale. "I have yet to see a shire. New or old."

"Oxo, quit it with the Brit talk," said Cameron. "You're not from here. We get it." He tossed the straw at Oxendale, and it bounced off his bony knee.

Everyone was analyzing the team results showing that we were third in the rankings, which was amazing considering we came from such a small town. Rankings factored in total fund-raising, and our town appeared to be very generous, when it came to that. When you added up our riders doing well in the challenges, winning even more in matching funds, our donation to the children's cancer research fund was going to be huge. That made me feel better about losing my phone. But not much.

After lunch, I asked Cameron if I could borrow his phone and found a private spot under a shady tree. I called Stella's number and crossed my fingers, hoping she'd been trying to call me and not getting through due to my misplaced phone.

Then again, she had been avoiding me for weeks. That probably wouldn't change in a day.

"Stella's phone," said a male voice.

"What? Is that Mason?" I said.

"Frances?" he replied. "Hey. Is everything okay?"

"Yes, fine. More or less," I said.

"What's this number? Why aren't you calling from your phone?"

"And why are *you* answering Stella's phone?" I teased back. Then it suddenly occurred to me that there might be a not-so-good reason for it, and I felt bad for laughing.

"Stella's busy. I'm in the waiting room."

"Which one?" I asked.

"Does it matter?" he complained. He sounded stressed out. "Sorry. We're at Mercy. They do outpatient stuff."

"Say hi to LaDonna for me?" I asked, referring to a nurse I'd recently met.

"Sure. So, what's up?" he asked.

I cleared my throat. "Well, here's the thing. I sort of lost my phone last night."

Mason laughed. "Sort of? How do you sort of lose a phone?"

"I'm not sure," I admitted. "I had it last night and I was

charging it, and then I was late getting up today and I started riding before I realized I didn't have it and—I guess I was tired—"

"You lost your phone. Seriously, Frances?"

"I know, I know."

"You can be spacey. Speaking of. What was up with you last night?"

"Up with me? Nothing, actually."

"Are you sure? You didn't sound like yourself."

"Who did I sound like?" I joked.

"You sounded delirious."

"Oh." How embarrassing. I'd drunk-dialed my best friend's brother. But I also knew it was no accident. I was getting more attached to Mason by the day. "I was super tired, just like you said. So, they're looking for my phone. Right now," I said. "It might be in our tent or my sleeping bag. I'm sure I'll find it when we unpack tonight. But if I don't . . . oh, never mind, I just hate not having it."

"What do you need one for?" he asked.

"Calling you, for example? I just feel so cut off from everything. And everyone."

"It's been, like, a few hours." He laughed. "What do you think you're missing? Anyway, you'll be home soon."

"I know, and I know you're going to think I'm 'just being Frances,' but do you think there's any way you could help me get a phone?"

"Me? Frances, I don't even know where you *are*," Mason said.

"You have the itinerary!" I protested. "We're at Sebago Lake right now and tonight we're going to be in Waterville, Watertown, something like that."

"Waterboro? That's like an hour and a half drive," Mason said. "Each way!"

"I know, I know, but—"

"Can't you just borrow someone's phone, like you're doing right now?"

"But what if . . . you know. Something important happens," I said. "Or an emergency."

"Sorry, but we're done with emergencies. I just—I don't need this right now." Mason sounded exasperated with me. "I mean, I don't know what you expect me to do. Drive there? With a new phone and everything? God, Franny. Sometimes you're so selfish."

I felt ridiculous all of a sudden. He was right. Why was I asking *him*? My mom would be here in a heartbeat if I asked her—after giving me a lecture on how much phones cost. But I didn't want to see her. I wanted to see him, I guess.

"It's okay," I said. "Sorry."

"I need to be here. I'm taking Stella to appointments, and doing stuff at the house. So I'm going to hang up now, and when Stella's done with her appointment, I'll tell her you called to say hi and you're doing fine. You'll call again to check on her. End of story." He ended the call abruptly, leaving me feeling about an inch tall.

When I looked up, I caught Margo's eye. It wasn't hard to do because she was standing there, apparently just waiting for me to get off the phone.

"Everything okay?" she asked.

"Sure," I said quickly.

"How's Stella?"

I'm not sure, actually. "She's doing well," I said.

I didn't give Margo a chance to ask any follow-up questions. I found Cameron over by the rest of the team and returned his phone, then stretched out on the ground to catch a few minutes of relaxation. When I closed my eyes, facing up, the sun made my eyelids orange-red. I thought about the time Stella and I went to a beach near Portland two summers ago, when we were fifteen, and how we'd insisted my mom sit somewhere else so we could look like we were on our own.

We'd lain faceup in the sun for so long that we'd both been sunburned to a crisp at the end of the day. Being on our own had meant forgetting to wear sunblock.

That was the summer Stella had a crush on Laird Offutt, who I insisted on calling Layered Outfit. He was very preppy, two years older than us, and she was convinced that they belonged together. He was going to be the captain of the boys' soccer team that fall, while Stella was a rising star on the girls' team. They trained together over the summer, and she was sure that they'd go to Homecoming together.

Instead, he went with a senior field hockey player named Muffy, and Stella and I stayed home and watched movies. Layered Outfit had horrible taste, we both decided. In clothes and in girls.

A foot nudged my side. "You ready to go?"

I looked up at Cameron, shielding my eyes from the sun. "What?"

"Come on, I'll ride with you. We can entertain ourselves by plotting how to break up Autumn and Alex."

"It can't be done," I said. "Besides, I don't care."

"You're so right. About both," Cameron agreed. "But come on anyway."

"We shouldn't." Cameron's chin rested on top of the fence rail.

"No," I agreed.

"It's wrong."

"It's *beyond* wrong," I said.

"But that one over there is asleep, and it would be so easy to just climb on, get a picture, and then jump off. Come on. Let's do it!" Cameron sounded more excited. "You get on Daisy over there and I'll sit on Elmer."

"You're naming them now?" I asked, smiling. "And who's going to take the pictures if we're both trying not to get thrown off by cows?"

"We'll get cow selfies. We'll send them to Stella. Wait till she sees we're not riding bikes, we're riding bovines."

"You go right ahead," I said. "The last time I got near a cow, something not so nice happened." I took off my helmet and ran my hands through my hair, shaking it out. Cameron and I had taken a slight detour, leaving the rest of the ride to follow the signs for the dairy farm. Why he wanted to see it, I wasn't sure.

When I climbed off my bike, my legs had that shaky, weak feeling I seemed to get every afternoon right around three p.m.

"Forget the cows. I'm going to start looking for a horse on this farm to take me the rest of the way today," I told Cameron, gazing around the large farm property.

Suddenly an image popped into my head: Stella, out

by the dairy farm. Stella, crumpled to the ground. My legs started to shake even more. I chugged some water.

Cameron laughed. "That would be incredible. Come on, let's leave our bikes here and go find someone we can talk to about that."

"We wouldn't . . . actually . . ."

"Why not?" he asked.

"Do you want the long version or the short version?" I said.

"Long." We strolled past the herd of cows lazing by the fence.

"We don't ride horses, as a rule. We have to finish every day's ride on our bikes—that's another rule," I said.

"Horse, cow, bike—what's the difference?" Cameron said. "They all end up giving you saddle sores."

"Can we *please* not talk about that?" I asked. I'd put in more than a hundred miles so far "in the saddle," and my body was not too happy about it.

Cameron pulled some long blades of grass and waved them through the fence, trying to get a cow's attention. "I see a problem with my plan. Once we got on one of these cows, would it even stand up? They look pretty lazy."

I looked over at him. "Wait a second."

"What?"

"The cows are lying down," I said.

"Is that like . . . code for something? The cows are lying down," he repeated in a deep voice. "The eagle flies at midnight. The red fox catches the brown mouse. Et cetera."

"When cows lie down, it means something!" I said.

"Yeah, it means they're too heavy to support themselves any longer," said Cameron. "It means they've been taking that growth hormone and it's made them all wacky."

"No. It means it's going to *rain*, dummy." I headed back for our bikes, taking a quick look at the sky. A few fairly ominous dark clouds were drifting overhead.

"What does 'raindummy' mean?" Cameron asked, following me.

"It means we should try to outride whatever's coming, or we're going to get drenched. Or worse."

"If you're talking about a thunderstorm, don't panic." Cameron swung his leg over his bike. "We're not going to get hit by lightning or anything."

I glanced up at the sky again. The dark clouds seemed to have increased already. "Maybe we should just stay here. We could, like, seek shelter at the barn."

"You could, like, have a point," Cameron said calmly as thunder crackled above us.

He was teasing me, in the middle of a severe storm. I got

on my bike, too, and we both started riding toward the barn, not sure if it would be open but hoping. The road was half dirt, half gravel, and as it started to rain, the ride quickly turned into a slow slog in the mud. Rain was falling in sheets, swooping as the wind blew sideways.

We rode up to a wide door opening, hopped off our bikes, and quickly ducked into the barn. It smelled like straw, manure, and dirt. I leaned my bike against a horse stall, and Cameron set his against a bale of hay.

We stood a few feet back from the doorway—I knew enough not to stand in a doorway when lightning was around. A boy in our junior high had been killed that way.

Rain was running off the roof in little streams, pooling into puddles just outside the door. Despite the storm, the air seemed to be getting hotter and more humid.

That was when I remembered it.

Dance in the rain or sleep under the stars. Or vice versa.

I pulled my shirt gently away from my stomach, and it made a slight sucking sound, like a wet bathing suit. My nylon super-fabric clothes were clinging to me, making me feel half-naked. *Yes, these are my exact curves and body proportions. Exactly.*

Not that there was anything about me in Cameron's imagination, but if there was, this meant there'd be nothing left *to* imagine. It wasn't exactly an ideal situation for me to be all confident and outgoing, but I had to try.

"So . . . this might sound silly, and I'm really not trying to make an, um, make an actual move or anything. But would you dance with me?" I asked.

"I told you. I don't dance." Cameron took a step away from me, a smile at the corner of his mouth. "And what do you mean that wasn't an *actual* move? I think that technically it was. What's with this dance obsession?"

"I'm not obsessed. I'm just trying to make the best of a bad situation." I wished I could tell him what I was up to; it wouldn't have been half as revealing or embarrassing.

I went outside, tentatively peeking around the corner to see if anyone was coming. Of course, why would they be? It was still storming, rain slashing at my face, although the thunder and lightning seemed to have passed.

How was a person supposed to start dancing on their own—in front of an audience of one? I thought back to the times I'd been nervous in recitals, the hokey phrases we told one another, like "Dance like nobody's watching," which made no sense to me. If no one was watching, why would I dance, and wouldn't I be really sloppy about it?

I started to move, slowly, gingerly, then pictured music in my mind, and old routines from the Shooting Sparks Dance

Company. We'd been a good team, really good. I was rusty, but it was like riding a bike: you didn't forget. I knew I wouldn't be able to take a picture for Stella, but I would describe the feeling, the moves, the way that even though raindrops were pouring down my body, I was somehow graceful.

It wasn't bad being outside in the pouring rain. It wasn't bad dancing again, either.

Why did I have to give up dance? I wondered. Just because Margo had been difficult to share the stage with, and because I was turning thirteen and self-conscious and because my mom was unemployed and money was tight, I'd told my mom I was done with it. That was easier than trying to make it work. But it had been something I really loved. I closed my eyes and looked up, feeling the rain on my face, washing all the dirt and sweat of the day's ride off me.

A clap of thunder suddenly boomed overhead, and it felt like the ground underneath me shook.

"Get in here!" Cameron reached out, grabbed my arm, and pulled me back into the barn.

We watched each other for a reaction, and I felt a small smile forming at the corner of my mouth. Then I burst out laughing, and he did, too.

"You're like a crazy person outside of school, aren't you?" he said.

"Pretty much," I said. Then I thought about it. "No, actually. The only person I act like this with is Stella. But I haven't even done that in front of her in a long time." I paused, looking at Cameron. "You know what's weird? Why weren't you and I friends before now? We share some classes, we live in the same neighborhood, and we probably take the same bus—"

"I ride my bike," Cameron interrupted me.

"All year? Even in the winter?"

He nodded.

"That sounds . . . painful. I'd never do that."

"You work at McDonald's," he said. "That sounds painful to me."

I laughed. "One person's pain is another person's . . . how does that go?"

He stared at me. "Never heard of it."

"Shut up, you have too," I said. "Anyway, we just—we're not on the same . . ."

"Team?" Cameron asked.

"Yes we are," I said.

"No, we're not," he said.

"Oh?"

"For one thing, you like to dance too much. I never knew you were so into it," he said.

"I wasn't. I mean, I'm not, but what can I say? This trip is making me do weird things."

"Yeah, well. For another, I'm pretty sure I'm gay. And that's not because of this trip, believe me."

"Oh," I said, finally getting it. "Wow. I'm sorry, I didn't know that."

"Why would you know? And don't be sorry—I'm fine with it," he said.

"No—I just meant I'm sorry that I was so clueless."

"When I was joking about you making a move . . . I mean, I hope you weren't really interested in me . . . that way," Cameron said. "I'd feel bad if I made you think something was, like, going on between us."

"No, it's cool," I said. "I actually need a friend right now more than anything else."

"So, we're cool?" he asked.

"Definitely," I said.

I was relieved. I liked Cameron and wanted to become better friends, but that was all. Over the past few days I'd begun to realize that I was thinking about Mason more and more. It seemed like wherever I went or whatever I did, there was something that made me think of him, and when I did, I'd have this mini-fantasy of seeing him when I got home, and of the two of us being together.

Fantasies are so unfair. It wasn't like he was going to be

interested in me. His little sister's best friend. The last time we'd talked, he'd called me selfish. That didn't bode well. The last time I'd seen him, he'd patted me on the head like I was a kindergartner.

"I don't mind if people know, but I'd rather tell them on my own. When I'm ready," said Cameron. "So if you don't mind kind of . . ."

"Not gossiping about you? Don't worry," I said. "I'm quite excellent at keeping things to myself."

Cameron and I rode up to the finish line later that afternoon. I was partially dry, but the humidity had kept me from completely drying out. My clothes were still sticking to me way more than I was comfortable with.

We coasted onto the soccer field where bikes were being stored and found our group's spot. We weren't the last to get there, and we weren't the first, from what I could see. We must have taken a shortcut—there was no other explanation, unless other people waited out the storm longer than we had. I stashed my bike on the wet grass. I couldn't wait to grab my stuff and go take a hot shower. I felt like a walking representation of sweat. Sweat personified.

We headed for the section of the field where our bags were waiting for us. I tossed my duffel over my shoulder and turned to head to the girls' showers while Cameron and Oxendale talked. I wandered toward the high school building and looked for the entrance so I could find the girls' locker room.

But there was someone leaning against a big sign by the school that said CCCR Riders—Locker Rooms Straight Ahead! and from a distance, I couldn't tell who. But as I got closer, I nearly keeled over, and not just from exhaustion.

"What are you doing here?" I asked Mason.

CHAPTER 9

I walked over to him and dropped my duffel. "Before you get all excited, I didn't bring you a new phone," he said. "I can't afford that. But I did bring you something we forgot to pack in your emergency bag." He held up a small square plastic box. "It's your patch kit."

"I have one of those," I said.

"I don't think so," he said. "I was the one who packed your saddlebag. Should we check it?"

"Sure, I . . . I guess." As I hoisted my duffel and led him over to the roped-off area where my bike was parked, I couldn't help wondering: did he really drive all the way for that? Seriously? After telling me off? Why didn't he just tell me he forgot it and that I should pick one up at the store or from a fellow rider?

Unless maybe he wanted to see me as much as I wanted to see him. But that was not likely. He didn't even trust me enough to have a patch kit.

We walked over to the bikes together, passing Margo, who was going the other way. She gave us an extremely curious look. I couldn't blame her. It didn't make sense that Mason was suddenly here.

"Hold on a second," Margo said, turning toward us. "Is Stella all right?"

"Oh, yeah, she's fine," I said. "He's my, uh, mechanic."

Mason waved the patch kit in the air as if it were important. Margo didn't look convinced, but we didn't stick around to chat any longer.

I found my bike and unzipped the small bag located under the seat. I rummaged inside and pulled out several things, but not a patch kit.

"See? I knew you needed one," said Mason. "And, I brought you extra socks. Except I left them in the truck."

"You brought me . . . socks," I said.

"Last week on one of our training rides, you were complaining about the clip-on shoes and how they rubbed your toes funny. So, these are made for biking. They have this material that resists sweat and improves your performance."

"My feet do not sweat," I said proudly. "And you're a cycling nerd."

"You're the one doing a three-hundred-and-fifty-mile bike ride," he replied, giving me a little push.

"Ouch. So, look, I really, really have to shower. Do you want to hang out for a while?"

"Sure, definitely," he said.

"Listen, I didn't want to say this, but I need to go to a store and buy some . . ." I leaned closer, about to say something really personal so he'd *have* to take me, but I decided on second thought that I didn't want to make it that embarrassing. "Shampoo," I said softly, instead. "My mom packed the worst kind for my hair."

"I can go get some and bring it back. . . ." he offered.

"No. No, you can't. You'll get the boy kind."

"There's a boy shampoo?"

"Shut up. Let me take a shower and then we'll go. As long as I'm back by dark, it'll be fine." That wasn't the rule, but it wasn't the time to stick to the rules. Not if I wanted to keep working on Stella's list.

"I'll wait here," Mason said. "Maybe you can borrow some

shampoo from someone, in the meantime?"

"You don't understand hair, do you? It's kind of tragic," I said.

"You're the one who's having a bad hair day. Not me." He pushed me toward the locker room.

Just before I went inside, I glanced back to see him sitting on a bench. Something was changing between us. But I was going to have to tell him about Stella's F-It List as soon as I washed my hair with crummy hair products and got dressed in clean clothes.

"We're not getting shampoo," I said as Mason and I drove away from the school, back down the same road that I'd covered on my bike earlier. "I mean, we are. But I have to do something else, too."

"Don't tell me. Conditioner."

"Ha-ha," I said. "No."

"So where are we actually going?" Mason asked as we headed across town.

I'd done some last-minute research on his phone while he drove. Lucky for me, there were sites with recommendations for tattoo and piercing salons in the middle of sort-of-southern Maine. Since I wasn't totally clear on where we were, it was all thanks to his phone's GPS.

"So, you have to promise me that you won't tell Stella about this. But she had this list of stuff she wanted to do on this bike trip," I said. "She talked about it all the time. She wanted us to do it together, but since she can't, I'm attempting to pull it off on my own. I'm doing it for her. Which means you have to take me to get a piercing."

"A what?"

"She wants to get her navel pierced," I said.

"She does?"

"She does, apparently. When she told me once, I thought she was joking. But see . . . she made this list. She talked about it a lot in the past couple of weeks—or, the weeks before the accident. Hold up—you can park here," I said, pointing to the small shop where we were headed.

Before we got out of the truck, I handed him the small green piece of paper. It was becoming worn and sweat-stained, because I never let it out of my sight.

"You . . . you're going to do all this?" Mason asked.

"Why do you sound so skeptical?"

He laughed. "You're afraid of heights. And you're not the type to parade around in a swimsuit, never mind a bikini. Do you even *have* a bikini?"

I felt my face getting warm, then hot as he looked at me. "There's a first time for everything," I said.

"Our old neighbors had a pool, and you wouldn't even go in without a T-shirt on," he reminded me.

"That's not true," I said. "Anyway, I'm trying to make a video or at least a photo book of everything I do for her." I shrugged. "Maybe it will make her laugh?"

"Maybe. That'd be a miracle." We paused outside the door of the Wing Nut Tattoo & Piercing Studio. "Maybe it will make *me* laugh."

"I doubt it," I said. "Since I'm the one getting it done, and you're the one with a phone, you have to take the video, and you hate needles."

Inside, the air-conditioning was on high. Too high. Like the chill would kill off any germs they might miss in the sterilizing process.

I did not want to shiver or even look chilled when I pulled up my T-shirt to reveal my belly button. I felt like too much of me was going to be exposed.

This would have been one thing if it were Stella. She's so in shape that she has those "cut" abs, a six-pack, I guess you could say.

I'd had one back in the day . . . while I was still on the dance team.

Since then, it was mostly just a stomach that went from flat to poochy to flat again, depending on the season and on whether I was exercising more than I was taking advantage of my meal discount at work. I have a weakness for Shamrock Shakes, and we were barely out of Shamrock Shake season.

But I didn't have time to worry about how I looked in front of a random tattoo artist or Mason. What was important was getting this done.

I'd made it through step one, which was getting my fake ID accepted. One night over Christmas break when Stella and I were bored and tired of not getting into R-rated movies, we'd attempted to create our own, but they looked truly amateur. They hadn't passed their first and only test at the Sparrowsdale Sixplex (which we were always calling the Sexplex). No, it wasn't that easy.

I'd ended up paying Liam Herzog-Williams fifty dollars for this one, which was a discounted rate that I'd negotiated only by swearing to recruit two more people who'd pay him for fake IDs over the summer. I was part of an evil, illegal pyramid scheme, basically. But it did the trick, and the fact that he'd given me a break on his usual price meant I still had a hundred dollars for the anonymous tip and enough money to pay for the actual piercing.

A woman with long black hair, 100 percent tattoo-covered arms and neck, and three piercings in her cheek, one through her nose, and two through her lip, sat down beside me. She was scary, but at least she knew what it was going to feel like.

"I'm Rhonda, and I'll be taking care of your body art," she said. "Can you verify your name and date of birth for me before I get started?"

"Sure." I told her the date I'd used on the form when I first arrived.

Rhonda opened a packet of fresh instruments, sort of like the ones I'd seen at the dentist. "You nervous? Don't be nervous," she told me, patting my arm. She looked over at Mason, who was standing off to the side. "You going to hold her hand?"

"Oh, uh, no." Mason shook his head. "I mean, she's fine. Total pro at this kind of stuff."

"Ha!" I laughed.

"Everything's sterile here, except maybe the language. Now, all I have to do is take this hollow needle here, and pull it through."

"Right. I've seen it done," I said. I'd Googled it. It was hard not to be nervous, though, with the sound of buzzing tattoo needles and the smell of singed flesh in the air.

Rhonda rubbed disinfectant on my navel. "Some people like to watch and some don't. I promise you, I'll be done as soon as I start. Now, you're going to have to take care of this when I'm done. I'll give you some ointment. You live around here?" she asked.

"No, I'm passing through on a bike trip," I said.

"A bike trip? You're kidding me. What kind of bike you have? Harley?"

"No, it's a . . . Trek," I said.

"Oh. Never heard of it."

"Bicycling," I said. "That kind of bike."

"No wonder!" She burst out laughing. "All done, Frances."

I glanced down at my stomach to admire the small silver-stud navel post I'd selected. Then I turned to Mason to see what he thought.

He was sitting on the floor, facing the opposite direction. "Mason?"

He waved without turning around. The back of his T-shirt looked a little dusty. He'd slid to the floor. I should have known. He couldn't do things like this.

I slowly sat up and hopped off the table. "Hey." I put my hand on his shoulder and tried not to acknowledge how different it felt to touch him this way instead of our usual fist bumps and playful shoves. "You going to be okay?"

He reached his hand up and covered mine with it. His touch made me shiver. It wasn't the extreme AC, either.

I crouched beside him, breaking our connection. "It's okay," I said. "I'm sorry. I shouldn't have asked."

"Don't be sorry. I got to see the whole thing," he said. "Well. Almost the whole thing."

I slowly stood and held out my arms to help him up. As I pulled him to his feet, there was a moment where he bumped into me. We lost our balance and awkwardly caught each other. "You need anything else while we're here?" Mason asked.

"Like . . . "

"A bike tattoo?" he suggested.

"No, let's quit while we're ahead," I said.

Then we strolled out of Wing Nut Tattoo & Piercing Studio, arm in arm, like it was something we did every day.

CHAPTER 10

"So is the piercing thing starting to hurt?" Mason asked as we drove back to the CCCR headquarters for the night.

After leaving Wing Nut, we'd grabbed a couple of burgers at a restaurant in town, and I was pretty sure I'd eaten like a ravenous animal. I didn't even remember eating my french fries, because I ate them so quickly. Mason didn't look shocked. He had to know how hungry someone would be after logging seventy miles on a bicycle. "No, it doesn't hurt at all," I said. "I don't think you have much actual feeling in your belly button."

"So I could punch you," Mason said, "and you wouldn't feel a thing."

"Don't push it. You only just started being nice by bring-ing me those socks."

"I know. But I wanted to see you," he said. "I mean, see how things were going. You sounded . . . I don't know. Lost."

"I kind of was," I said. "You saw the list. You can probably guess what I tried to do last night."

"Drink something stronger than water?" he guessed.

"Oh yes. And let me tell you. That's something I don't need to do again." I shuddered, thinking of the bitter taste and the headache it had given me that morning. "Do you . . . ever? I mean, you're in college, so you probably go to a lot of parties."

"Not really." He downshifted the truck as we turned into the high school parking lot. We parked in a far corner, away from the field of eighty-plus tents. Mason turned off the engine, but neither one of us made a move to get out.

"We have a pretty intense code of conduct for the hockey team," he explained. "We have to keep a certain GPA, we can't do anything illegal—I mean, obviously. Some guys try to get around it, but I don't. It's not worth it. I have a scholar-ship, you know?"

"I guess I remember that." I thought about the high school hockey games Stella and I had gone to when he played—we'd ostensibly be there with her parents to support Mason, but we'd spend our time laughing with friends instead of watching the game, and checking out the guys from the other school.

"So are you missing school right now?" I asked. The sky was getting dark, which was our official time to turn in for the night. "Is that okay?"

Mason nodded. "For now. I decided to take a leave of absence for a while. Since hockey's over for the season, it's okay with my coach. This way I can help my parents, help Stella."

"Wow. That's so admirable of you. That's a big sacrifice."

"You sound surprised that I would do it," he said. "Am I that horrible?"

"No, I didn't mean it like that! I'm in awe, actually."

"It's okay, taking a break. I'm not really sure what I want to major in, and I don't want to take the wrong classes, you know? They said I can make up what I miss by taking some summer classes."

"How can classes be wrong?" I asked.

"Well, I started out in economics. Now, though, I want to do something more hands-on, like becoming a vet."

"A vet? But . . . you'd have to cut open cute little kitties," I said. "How could you do that?"

"It's not all surgery," he said. "And I'd be *helping* them.

But you may have a point. I should probably look for some-thing that doesn't involve knives and bodies."

"You sound scary right now," I teased him.

"I could be a radiologist. Just look at cute little kitty X-rays. I don't know. Why, what do you think you're going to do?"

"Me? I really have no idea," I said. I opened the door and slid out.

"You should start thinking about it," he said, walking around the truck toward me.

I scuffed the ground with my flip-flops. I wasn't ready to think, or talk, about the future right now. I'd always hoped Stella and I would go to the same college or university— how else would I graduate? (I'm only half joking.) I knew we could find a school we both wanted to attend. But now what? Would things be different?

"I should probably go," he said, "and you should probably get back before people notice you're gone."

"It's like a jailbreak," I said, smiling.

We walked across the parking lot. We were both moving really slowly. I knew I didn't want the night to be over. I didn't want him to leave and go back to Sparrowsdale without me. On the other hand, I had to stay and finish this thing. I only had four days to go.

We were almost to the edge of the tents when he said, "I left the socks in the truck. You want to come with me?"

"Sure," I said.

We walked back to the truck, a little quicker in this direction. My leg muscles were beginning to feel sore and tired. My back was kind of aching, and I had a pinched feeling in my stomach.

Oh, right, I realized. *It's my new accessory.*

"I can't believe I almost left without giving you these." Mason unlocked the passenger-side door and reached for a package behind the seat. "How stupid can I be? Don't answer that."

"I'm the one who lost my phone. I think we're both a little preoccupied," I said.

"Speaking of which, do you want my phone? I'll give it to you for the rest of the trip," he offered.

"What? No, that's okay."

"No, really. I'd feel better if you took it," he said.

"Thanks, that's really generous. But I'll be fine," I said.

"Are you sure? You can stay in touch with Stella that way. It's new. Check it out." He handed me the phone and gave me a quick rundown of the features it had. He went on and on about them, as if this were the first smartphone ever invented, as if I was going to take it and needed instruction. He was leaning close to me, almost into me. Our ears were touching. How can a stupid ear be sexy? But it was.

Oh God, if you don't feel the same way and don't kiss me right now, I'm going to die, I thought.

But I could never say anything like that to him. I had to just take the orange socks and get back to my tent. Soon.

"So you really don't want this?" he asked.

"Want . . . ?"

"This phone," he said, not moving.

"Right," I said in a slightly hoarse voice that didn't even sound like me. I could hardly breathe. I was going to do that embarrassing thing where you literally choke on air. I hate when I do that thing. Like, who doesn't remember to breathe correctly?

"Frances? You're really beautiful, you know that?" Mason reached out and pushed back a stray curl of my hair, one of the short layers that always fell into my face that I'd tried to grow out and never succeeded at. His hand lingered on me for a second. He ran his fingers down the side of my cheek. Before I could make a move toward him, he kissed me.

After a minute he pulled back, gently brushing at my lips with his fingers. "Sorry, I—"

"No, it's okay. Keep doing that," I said, leaning back in for more.

Suddenly the F-It List popped into my mind. *Have an epic kiss.* This was happening. Something about Mason and this epic kiss made me feel like I was a different person than I'd been a couple of weeks ago. Like I was older, no longer just Franny but actually Frances, someone growing into her name. Someone who had feelings for her best friend's older brother because of everything we'd been through together lately.

We smushed a little closer together, still kissing, and as he reached for my waist, his wrist brushed my new piercing. "Ouch!" I said, but as soon as the pinched feeling started, it was over.

"Sorry. Does it hurt a lot?" Mason asked, backing up a little.

"What?"

"Your belly button."

"No." I shook my head. "It's fine."

"I thought you said it had no feelings."

"Apparently it does," I said.

Then we kind of attacked each other all over again.

"Um, should we be doing this?" I stepped back, wondering if I should stop now. I should get back to . . . wherever it was. Wherever I was supposed to be and whoever I was. But now it was getting really dark, and I didn't want to leave Mason. "I mean . . . I want to do this."

"So do I," he said.

We kissed some more and then he opened the truck passenger door again, and we both just climbed in together and kept kissing. This was crazy. Insane. But great. It just felt so good to be with someone who knew what was actually going on in my life and who understood. We were both scared, I could tell that. We were both terrified. But we were in it together.

"It's getting late," he whispered into my neck. "You should probably go find your tent."

"I know," I said. But I wasn't going anywhere.

I was brushing my teeth the next morning when Margo walked into the locker room. For once, I was ahead of her, but only because I'd been awake since five a.m.

She glared at me. "I thought you *left* last night," she said. "I thought you ruined it for everybody."

I finished brushing and rinsed my mouth. "I'm still here," I said. "What would I ruin?"

"But first I saw you with Mason, then you weren't at dinner, and then you weren't in the tent when we were supposed to be. What did you do? Did you go off somewhere with him or what?" she asked.

"Not that it's any of your business, but I came back to the

tent a little after five. I was here the whole time. I just . . . fell asleep in his truck."

"Yeah, right. How dumb do you think I am? I didn't know you and he, I mean . . . are you and he together?"

"No." I shook my head. But then I thought, *yes*, and *I don't know*. Mason was an incredible person, but he was nineteen and I was seventeen, and I thought he was probably too old for me, but it didn't actually feel that way, not ever and definitely not after the night we'd spent being close. I couldn't stop asking myself questions like, *What was that? Why was he here? Did we just do that because of Stella, because we're both worried and freaked out?*

Margo left, and I leaned against the wall in the entryway to the locker room. So much had happened in the past couple of days—in the past couple of weeks. I wasn't quite sure how to handle it all.

When I walked out, thoughts swirling in my head, Heather, the ride director, was waiting for me. "I need to talk to you," she said. "Can you come with me for a sec?"

It wasn't a question. It was an order.

I followed her to a picnic table, a secluded area. All I could think was that she was going to tell me that I'd been riding too slowly. Too often. They were taking away some of the money Sparrowsdale had raised—because of me, the weak link in the chain.

"Frances, I'm sorry," Heather said when we found a bench where we could sit down. "But we can't let you stay on this trip. You broke one of our most important rules. You're going to have to leave tonight. Who can come pick you up?"

"Please, you can't kick me off the trip. Please!" I begged. "What did I do? What did I do?"

"Last night you didn't stay in your tent with your team. We have strict rules about male and female interaction. We have guaranteed certain things to parents, to teachers, to *you*. This isn't a trip to take if you want to hook up."

"I didn't want to hook up!" I cried. I mean, maybe in the moment, sure, but I wouldn't tell her that. "I didn't go into this trip thinking *that*. I had no intention of ever—"

"Nobody ever does," Heather said. "You signed an agreement, saying you'd abide by the rules. And the rules apply to everybody."

"You have no idea how important this ride is to me. Please. I'm doing this ride because my friend can't. Stella's injuries . . . they're more serious than she wants people to know. I mean, she's not even telling me half of it, but the half I know is pretty bad. She's barely even herself anymore. She's mad at everyone, she's mad at the world . . . she's mad at me. So if there was one thing I could do to try to help—it was completing this ride in her place. That way all her donations will count."

"I'm sorry to hear that. Wow. I don't know what to tell you," Heather said. "I know Stella, and I know your dropping out would probably crush her, because it would also mean disqualifying your team."

"You'd disqualify the whole *team*? No, that can't happen!"

"You broke our rules. In any other circumstance, this would be grounds for dismissal." She tapped her fingers together.

Wait a minute. She'd said, "In any other circumstance." That sounded slightly hopeful. She looked like she was thinking of some other punishment for me. Did she realize that having me ride four more days was, in a way, already punishment?

"I'm trying to think of another solution. Your team could stay, but they'd need another rider, and you've already made it this far," Heather mused. "That seems unfair to make them accountable for your actions. But if I let this pass without any action on my part, I don't know how we can ask others to respect the rules."

"You could not tell them what happened?" I said.

She just gazed at me over her sunglasses, like that was the dumbest thing she'd ever heard. I had to say something else to convince her. Something good.

"I—if it helps? We didn't, like, *do* anything," I said.

Her face turned slightly red, as if she didn't need that information and wished I hadn't shared.

"I know this is embarrassing," I continued, "but honestly, we just sort of cuddled—"

"I get the picture," she said, cutting me off. "I'm not sure it helps me with this decision. Give me some time to talk with my team. You, go meet with your team at your staging area. I'll come find you and give you the answer. There may be conditions involved, just so you know."

I nodded, eager to accept any and all conditions. "Of course, of course. Whatever you think is best. But please, please, don't make me go home. I know I'm not the best rider here, but it means a lot to me to finish this, and the same goes for Stella. More than you could know."

I wandered off, in a daze, stunned that I might have blown this entire thing. I should have known I couldn't stay out late with Mason; when he asked if I should go, I should have said *Yes, I guess so,* and pulled away.

But I hadn't been able to make myself do that, not when he and I were discovering we had such strong feelings for each other.

How had Heather found out that I wasn't back in the tent by lights-out, though? Weren't we on an honor system with our own team?

I walked back to my team at the staging area and went straight to Margo, pulling her aside so not everyone could hear. "You *told* on me?"

"Told on you what?" she asked.

"Last night. How I didn't sleep in the tent the whole night."

"I didn't—why would I do that? Why should I care where you sleep?" she muttered.

"You cared about ten minutes ago. And if you didn't tell Heather, then how else did she know?" I asked.

"They do a tent check every night, probably. They should, if they're responsible. I don't know, why don't you ask Autumn and Elsa if they said something?" Margo asked.

"Because. Why would they care where I was or if I was doing something wrong? No, it has to be you."

"What are you two arguing about now?" Autumn asked, coming closer. "Are you both ready to go? Because we'll be taking off soon. Don't you need to change?" she asked me.

"I'm—well. I'm half-changed," I said. "I'll get my bag."

"Yeah, that's if you even need it," said Margo.

"Why would she not?" asked Elsa in a wispy voice.

"You're not giving up, are you?" said Autumn. "Oh my God. You are giving up. You're going to ruin this *now*, when we're almost halfway there?"

"Are you hurt, is that it, Fran?" asked Oxendale.

"I'm not giving up!" I said. "And I—I'm not injured." I glanced over at Cameron, my closest friend on the trip. He wasn't coming to my defense. Before I could explain further, Heather walked over and stood in front of us. "Frances, may I have a word?" she said.

I held my breath as we moved out of the way, finding a little privacy by one of the breakfast tables. Heather cleared her throat. This was awkward for her too, no doubt. "While I in no way want to condone your rule breaking, I've consulted with my colleagues, and we've decided to let you stay on the ride."

"Oh, thank you!" I gasped.

"But there will be strict conditions, Frances. One, you need to check in with us every night. Whether you're coming or going, we need to know. Two, once you're in for the night—and it's lights-out—you can't leave the tent under any circumstances. Unless it's to use the restroom, I suppose, and if you do that, you'll need to have one of your tent mates accompany you. I'll be talking to them as well, but not right now—I have too much to do."

I nodded. That was embarrassing. "I really am sorry. I've never been under, like, this much stress before. Between the ride and Stella and . . . I made a bad decision. It's not like me. You have no idea. I'm not that kind of person, usually," I added.

"It's my responsibility to keep all of you safe. And accounted for," Heather said. "That's all I care about right now."

"Got it," I said. "I won't give you any more trouble, as far as that's concerned."

Heather didn't look impressed by my promises. "We'll see," she said, and briskly walked away to the group of volunteers who were checking in by the support vehicles.

I let out a huge sigh of relief and went back to my bike. Somehow I was down to one bike bottle; I had no idea where I'd left the other one. Maybe in Mason's truck? I didn't have time to think about it. I had to grab my clothes and finish getting dressed. I'd need to get my back-up water bottle, too—it was a travel mug from Mercy Hospital.

I was halfway through getting my clothes to go change when I remembered: today was the day I'd planned to do the most awful item of the F-It List. I had to wear a bikini, instead of my usual shirt and baggy shorts.

This wasn't a good day for it. Everyone hated me, and I was on shaky ground.

But if you looked at it another way, things couldn't get much worse. If I went ahead and got this over with on the day when nobody wanted to associate with me, that might have its advantages. If I was going to be exiled, why not be exiled on the most embarrassing day of all?

I'm not rail thin like Autumn or Margo or most of the other riders were. I have curves. And I don't do bikinis in front of three hundred people. If I'm hanging out at a neighbor's pool? Sure—despite what Mason said about my always wearing a T-shirt. That might have happened once or twice when I was twelve, but not since.

What if I wore the bikini top *under* my shirt—would that count? No. Probably not.

But there was no way I was giving up my padded shorts to wear only a bikini bottom. I already had saddle sores. I'd compromise by wearing my shorter pair of bike shorts and rolling the waistband down a bit to show off my belly button. That would have to count.

"You're getting your stuff ready. Does that mean you're not kicked off?" Margo asked.

"I'm still on the trip," I said.

"Wait a second. You almost got us kicked off the ride?" asked Oxendale. "What did you do?"

Suddenly all seven other riders were circled around me. It felt like an inquisition. I had to talk fast or they might shoot me—that was how they looked.

"I broke a rule," I quickly admitted. "It's not a super-big deal. I talked to Heather and it's going to be okay. I just have to check in with her more often." *And not spend the night with Mason again.* Which would be easy. He was gone. Unless of course he came back tonight, too, which would be awesome. . . .

"What rule?" Autumn asked.

"I—well—see—Stella's brother, Mason, we were talking," I said. I couldn't confess to the rest of it in front of all these people; I hadn't even told my best friend yet. "The time got away from us, and I ended up falling asleep in his truck. I broke the tent curfew."

Nobody said anything for a minute. Then Cameron asked, "How could you be so stupid? Don't you know how long we've worked for this, how much is at stake? Maybe *you* don't care, but we're trying to make a difference here."

"I know. I'm sorry." I looked down, embarrassed. "Yes. It was really dumb. I promise I . . . I'm in this thing to finish."

Somehow it didn't matter that I'd talked my way into stay-ing. Everyone hated me anyway.

They went back to getting their bikes ready, and I headed for the locker room to change. Margo trailed along beside me. "Now you have two strikes against you. One, you're the last one to finish every day. And two, you almost cost us the trip. You're on thin ice."

"Which is it?" I asked, annoyed. "A baseball metaphor or a skating metaphor? Because I'm confused."

She stopped walking. "You know what? I've been trying to help you. But you're on your own from here on out."

"Help me? You?" I laughed.

I left her and went into a locker room stall to get changed. When I came out, she was gone. Outside, everyone was lining up for the start.

I tried to keep a low profile, which wasn't easy in a hot-pink bikini top, with platinum hair and a pierced navel. This was getting ridiculous.

As I got on my bike and slowly rode over to the start, Max and Oxendale zipped past in a blur, followed by Autumn and Alex in their practically matching outfits. If they noticed me, they didn't say anything.

I worked my way up in the crowd of cyclists and stopped to adjust my seat a bit. This wasn't the day to ride in a bikini top. It really wasn't. I made sure I had everything I'd need for what was going to be a hard day: water, the patch kit (Mason), extra socks (Mason), extra shirt, and the hundred-dollar bill I was carting around in my bike bag every day.

Suddenly I spotted Cameron off to the side, and I gradually made my way over toward him. I bumped his back wheel and he turned to look at me.

"What's with the getup?" he asked.

I wished I had something, anything, even a giant peach dress to cover me. "It's a dare, actually. Can you get a photo for Stella?"

"Maybe later!" he called as the horn sounded and he took off, at a pace I'd never be able to catch up with.

So it was going to be like that.

Well, maybe I deserved it.

After a few minutes on the road, the long line of riders stretched out, as we all got into our normal riding paces. Translation: Frances at the back.

Ride in the Back. No One Will Notice Your Screwups.

Ride in the Back. Nobody Will See You in a Bikini.

After a minute, I noticed Elsa riding beside me. Thank goodness for Elsa. She'd stick with me. She'd been nothing but supportive during this whole journey so far. She might not say much, but she was rooting for me, I could tell.

I turned and gave her a small smile. "It's for Stella," I explained. "The outfit. Do you think you could get a photo for me?"

"Sure." She took out her phone, focused it on me, and clicked the camera button.

"Thank you so much. I promised her a travelogue of the trip."

"It's okay. Good luck," she said softly, and then she took off with a sprint.

Well. So much for companionship. I was on my own.

I lowered my shoulders and focused on getting a good cadence going with my pedals, a strong, steady, rhythmic pace I could keep up for hours. I tried to ignore the slight pulsing feeling in my belly button.

Three more days after today. That was all I had to do. Three more days and I could see Stella again.

Three more days and I could see Mason again, too.

Stella, Mason, Stella, Mason, I thought as my legs pushed the pedals.

I didn't know what Stella would think of me and Mason being together. She might not be a fan. On the other hand, she might think it was a good idea. It would depend on a lot of things, like whether Mason felt the same way about me as I felt about him. Maybe it was a one-time thing that would never happen again.

Thinking about him now, I didn't want that to be true. I loved the way it felt when we were curled up together. I loved kissing him. I loved how he played with my hair, pushing the curls behind my ear, out of the way when we kissed, holding me close.

But if it made Stella uncomfortable or angry, I wouldn't pursue anything with Mason. She had enough to deal with.

CHAPTER 12

That afternoon, the road was shimmering ahead of me, the way Cameron had once warned me it would.

Surprisingly, my legs felt okay, and my mind was focused, but I felt like I was about to pass out from sunstroke. I could tell that my shoulders were getting sunburned—it wasn't like I'd had time to put on sunscreen. I also thought—no, I knew—I was lost.

I didn't know how I'd gone wrong, whether I took a wrong turn or just wasn't paying attention, or was I so far behind it didn't matter? But that was where the sag wagon was supposed to be—behind the last person. So I wasn't on the right path anymore. I hadn't been since lunch, when I'd taken off without the group, since they weren't speaking to me, anyway. I hadn't eaten much, because I was too distracted, thinking of Stella, and Mason, and how much everyone else was angry with me.

I stopped for a minute beside the road, leaning my bike against the slight hill. I had to get back on course quickly so I could check in with Heather at the end of the day's ride, or I'd forfeit the ride that I'd just argued to keep. I rode slowly—half out of necessity and half out of hope that someone else would come by. I drank some water and wiped sweat from my forehead with the "magic shirt" Stella had told me to keep in my bike bag—the one time she'd felt like talking to me about the ride.

That's what she called it. Her magic shirt. A long-sleeved thin, black "technical" T-shirt that collapsed into what felt like a tiny scrap of fabric, so you could carry it with you in your saddlebag and it didn't add any weight. She'd given me special instructions when she handed it over, as if it were a holy garment. "There's nothing worse than getting drenched with sweat and then going down a long downhill and freezing. So keep this shirt with you, and you can always swap it out for the wet one," she'd told me.

One of the few times she'd talked to me.

There were worse things than a sweaty shirt. Much worse. As we'd recently learned.

As I held out the so-called magic shirt to examine it and let the wind dry it out a bit before putting it on, I contemplated that it was more like a suggestion of a shirt. It was an arm's worth of fabric, and maybe that would fit Stella, but it would never fit me. Still, I was desperate.

I put the black shirt over my bikini top because I was getting sunburned, and knowing Stella, this shirt had some massive SPF rating that would protect me. I should have thought of it sooner.

The fabric snagged on my new belly-button stud. I'd disinfected it at least five times since the night before, but I was still worried it'd become a problem. Well, it was a problem. My mom would kill me when and if she found out about it.

Now the magic shirt was all sweaty, but so was I, so who cared? The last magic thing I'd put on had been that awful peach prom dress. Which, come to think of it, was not magic, and was still stuffed in the trunk of my mom's car. I couldn't stand to take it out and return it to the store. I owed Flanberger's something for it, but I just couldn't make myself deal with it because of what else had happened that day.

Every morning they gave us little maps to store in our saddlebags, in case this happened, in case we went off track.

There was a problem with this plan: I was—and still am—horrible at reading maps. If I didn't know where I was, then how could I figure out how to get where I should be? That was too deep to contemplate while I was lost. I unfolded the map, studied it as best I could. We'd crossed from Maine into New Hampshire before lunch, and were supposed to be riding into Concord, the capital, by the end of the afternoon. But no sign I'd seen recently had anything to do with Concord. We were taking lots of back roads because they were safer and had more room for large groups. But now I was a single, solitary rider and I felt deserted.

I decided to just keep riding in the same direction and see if I got to any of the roads that were listed. If a car passed by, I might attempt to flag it down. Or I might chicken out because I'd been taught never to flag down cars. For any reason.

I looked up at the sun but couldn't see it through the mostly cloudy sky. Even if I could, how much would that help me? The sun rose in the east, set in the west, and it was the middle of the afternoon, so . . . I was somewhere between point A and point B, riding twelve miles an hour, at least according to the little computer thing on the handlebars. If I got this question in Algebra 2, I would have nailed it. I always nailed the math word problems. But I needed more information first.

If only I hadn't lost my phone.

I kicked the ground, the pavement, scuffing the clippie shoes with their masking-tape messages from Mason. I knew I couldn't give up, but I wanted to.

I climbed back on the bike and pedaled for a while. I came to an intersection, and the crossroad had more cars on it than the road I was on, so I turned right. After a while the road said I was going south, which boded well, so I kept going, my muscles burning as I climbed a hill that would have been at home at a ski area. In the Alps.

As I finally crested the hill—using the "granny gears" to get there—my eyes widened. There was a little café on the side of the road. As I got closer, I pedaled harder. Maybe this was an oasis, but if it was, it sure had a lot of trucks parked outside.

As I coasted up, a tall woman with short white hair was closing the door, with her key in the lock. "Wait!" I cried. "No!"

She looked over her shoulder at me. "Can I help you?" She had a traditional, sort of old-fashioned pink waitress uniform on, the kind you see in old diner illustrations or on MeTV. She was wearing the kind of shoes that nurses wore—bright white and rubbery-looking.

"Please," I said, stepping off the bike. "I'm lost. And I

have to get back on course, and I'm out of water and—"

"Come on in," she said as she examined the number pinned to my shorts. "You're doing the Cure Childhood Cancer Ride? I heard that was passing near here—comes close from year to year."

"Near here. That's the problem," I said. I glanced at the trucks in the parking lot. They all had For Sale signs in their windows. The other business at the same place was Dewey's Trucks—New and Used and Spare Parts.

So the café wasn't crowded with guests, like I'd thought. It really was closing.

"We close at three, but—"

"What time is it?" I asked.

"Two fifty-eight. We haven't had a customer in a while—we're mobbed until one—so I was sneaking out early. I'm glad you caught me, though. You look a little worse for wear, no offense."

"Oh, I know I do," I said. "I'm doing all right, though. I just got lost and—I wasn't wearing the right clothes. Actually, I'm still not wearing them."

"You look beat." She guided me to a seat at the counter of what looked like an old diner, one that had been here for eons, with metal counter stools that twirled when you sat down. I held on tight so I wouldn't fall. My legs had hit the midafternoon wobbly stage. She handed me a cold, wet wash-cloth for my face, and I cleaned grit and sweat off my neck, face, and arms. When I was done, I noticed she'd placed a large red plastic glass of water in front of me. "Where are you from?"

"Sparrowsdale," I said. "It's north of North Conway?"

"Sure, sure. I know it. What do you need to eat?" she asked, catching me staring at the dessert case behind her. "I've got a nice blueberry cake—it's not too heavy. And then I'll make some calls for you?" she offered, getting the cake with one hand and the phone with the other.

I admired her balancing skills. "No," I said. "I mean, no thanks, you can't call anyone for me. I have to do this on my own. But, um, I would love a small piece of cake."

She cut a hunk and served it on a little plate, where it hung over the edges. As good as the food had generally been on the trip, this was better by far. "You know what you need with blueberry cake? Lemonade," she said, pouring a short glassful and sliding it over next to my giant cup of water. "By the way, my name's Miranda. What's yours?"

"Frances," I said. "I know you have to leave soon, but maybe you could point me in the right direction?" I unfolded the small crumpled map and spread it out on the counter.

Miranda studied it for about fifteen seconds. "Number

one, you're not that far off course. Number two, you took the hard way. You've got a bit of sidetracking to do and you'll find the right spot," she said.

"Really?" I couldn't believe it. Things were suddenly not as bad as they had seemed fifteen minutes ago. Quite the opposite, actually. We went over the map together as I ate the cake and rehydrated.

"I should probably get going," I said after a few minutes. "I'm already pretty far behind."

"Okay, then. Why don't you bring in your water bottles and we'll fill them up," said Miranda. "One with water, one with lemonade."

I tiptoed out of the diner on my bike shoes, as they made that obnoxious *clip, clip* sound on the floor. I sounded a little like a horse. Or, like a little horse. I wasn't sure. I grabbed my two containers and brought them back inside.

Miranda quickly filled my clear water bottle, and then she started to pour lemonade into my Mercy Hospital travel mug. "Christmas travel mug, huh? I got a ton of Christmas mugs. Every year someone brings me another, like I work in a diner so coffee mugs must be my favorite thing." She rolled her eyes. "Real original."

"Yeah. It's actually not a Christmas mug," I said. "It says, or it's supposed to say, Mercy. For Mercy Regional."

"Oh. Does someone you know work there? That how you got it?" she asked.

"No." I shook my head.

She waited for me to say more. She kept scrubbing a chrome napkin holder, although it looked perfectly clean to me.

"A nurse gave it to me. She was trying to comfort me by giving me some tea. I had just found out about my friend— my best friend. She was in an accident." I couldn't go into detail, I couldn't go back to that day and think about it. "So I'm doing this ride for her," I explained. "For my friend Stella, who signed up in the first place."

Miranda stopped polishing. She slowly slid the Mercy cup toward me, across the counter. "I'm sorry to hear that."

I traced the fancy script letters in the Mercy logo. Mercy. Merry. It really depended on how you looked at it, whether you viewed it from one side or the other.

"I've worked here a long time, and I was married a long time. I've seen a lot of things. And if there's one piece of advice I can give you, it's to enjoy the time you do have with someone," said Miranda. "Make the most of it. Might sound corny or overused, but it's the damn truth. Now, about your friend. Did she make it?"

"Oh yeah, she made it. I mean, she's okay," I said. *Kind of but not really.*

"So hurry up and finish this ride. That's my advice." She put the cake back in the dessert case and slid the door closed. "Not very original, I'm afraid."

"That's okay," I said. "It helps."

What didn't help was all the things this conversation was making me think about.

How badly off Stella was.

How much her life was going to change.

I couldn't stop wondering, was she going to do the stuff we used to do or would everything be different now?

"Do you think I could use the restroom quick?" I asked. Miranda nodded, and I went into the ladies' room to wash my face. I stayed in there a few minutes, running cold water over my wrists and splashing it on my neck, trying to keep myself from breathing so quickly. It felt like I was having a panic attack, not that I'd actually had one before. I took deep breaths and ran a cold paper towel across my forehead.

The ladies' room was tiny, to the same scale as the small diner café. I looked at myself in the mirror: sunburned neck, bright bikini top under a thin black top, wrinkled race number pinned to my short bike shorts, a pierced belly button, and a line of bike grease stretching from my elbow to my wrist. I was a wreck, but Miranda had treated me like I was just another customer.

I reached into the small back pocket of my shorts, the only pocket with a zipper. I took out the hundred-dollar bill that Stella had made me promise to leave for someone unsuspecting. If I tried to give it to Miranda, she'd reject it—I was sure of it. But if I left it in the bathroom, how would I know she would be the one to get it?

I searched under the sink for something I could hide it in, but then, how would I get her the message to look? This was too complicated.

Hiding the bill in my fist, I walked back out to the counter, where she was restocking silverware, her back to me. I quickly slid the folded bill under my cake plate, which she'd left on the counter—probably waiting to see if I wanted another piece. She was that nice.

"I'm going to take off," I announced. "Thank you so much for everything."

"You sure you don't want me to give you a ride to Concord? I don't have much time—have to pick up my grandson from day care at four, and unfortunately his day care's in the opposite direction, but I think—"

"Thanks, but no. I'd be breaking the rules. It's something I have to do on my own," I said.

She followed me outside to where my bike was leaning against the front window. "Nice bike," she commented. "I love silver."

"Thanks for your help. This has been one of the high points of the ride," I said. "If not the high point."

"Well, we are on a hill," she said, laughing. "I'm going to run inside and clean up a little bit more. You have a good ride, now." She went over the directions with me one more time. "Remember, hurry up and finish this thing so you can spend time with your friend—what's her name?"

"Stella," I said.

"Nice name. Give her my best wishes. You two ever end up on a road trip, drop by. I'll be working at this place till I'm ninety." She gave me a small wave as I donned my helmet and took off down the road. I had to ride fast, had to clear the area before she went in and found that hundred-dollar bill.

I had an hour and a half to get my butt to the meeting place in Concord. If I wasn't there, Heather wouldn't be as understanding this time around. I was already on thin ice, as Margo had pointed out oh so kindly.

One good thing about having gone *up* such a huge hill in the first place was that I got to coast down the other side of it. I released my hold on the brakes and let the bike pick up speed. I was dropping fast, soaring down the mountain.

Fly like you mean it, Mason had told me, and I was flying. I crouched down into aerodynamic mode, cradling the handlebars, feeling the cold air rush over my back. I glanced at the computer on my handlebar as my speed went higher and higher. Suddenly, at the bottom of the hill, the pavement changed from smooth to bumpy and my tires bounced on the uneven surface, radiating pain up my arms and nearly jolting me off the bike. I struggled to stay on like a bronco rider in a rodeo.

Then I hit a pothole, my front tire slamming into the crater, jarring my teeth with a cringe-inducing bump.

CHAPTER 13

I got off the bike on the side of the
road, heart pounding, out of breath.

I hadn't crashed. And thank goodness no cars had been
near me when it happened.

But my front tire was losing air, and as I stood there,
recovering, it slowly sank down to nothing. It was completely
flat.

I didn't know how to fix a flat tire. At all.

I knew I should, but I didn't. I knew it was one of the
things Mason and his dad had gone over with me, one of the
"Need to Know" items that I'd practiced once. But honestly,
there were a lot of those items—too many. I hadn't paid that
much attention, because I knew there would be a support

vehicle or two who would be on the scene when I ran into mechanical problems like this.

Unless, of course, I got lost and was nowhere near a support vehicle.

I started thinking about who I could call, who could walk me through it.

I could call Mason, but that would open up a can of strange worms. Like, did I really need him to come to my rescue all the time? That was setting up a weird precedent. It wasn't true, anyway. Or at least it wasn't *all* true.

I could call Stella, but she'd probably be so annoyed by me. Did she really need to know I had a flat tire and was in the middle of, well, nowhere? To be clear, I wasn't lost anymore. But neither was I on the right road.

I could call my mom, who would immediately initiate some rescue plan that involved helicopters and ambulances.

Then I remembered I didn't have a phone. Fantasy over. Reality setting in.

For once, Frances, rely on yourself. It's a flat tire. Nothing more, nothing less.

I stared at the front wheel. "Why did you have to go hit that pothole, anyway?" I mumbled. "You should have seen it coming. And what are you made out of, glass?"

I was losing it. I was talking to my bike now.

I ran my hand around the wheel. First I had to take it off the bike. There was a quick-release lever for that, so I flipped it to the open position and then pulled at the wheel. It didn't come off. I tried a few more times. Nothing.

This wasn't going well.

I cursed a few times as I battled the wheel—then suddenly, I remembered another part of Mason's instructions. *Don't forget to release the brake, too.*

Right. The stupid brake. Once I did that, I wrestled the wheel off and leaned it against a tree. I was well off the road, because the last thing I wanted was to be close to any traffic while I did this.

I knew I had to peel the tire off the rim. That was the second step. I got the little patch kit out of my saddlebag and a green plastic lever-like thing that looked like a bike tool, and whether it went with this kit or it was the thing my mom had given me, I couldn't even tell anymore.

I slowly, deliberately worked the lever around the edge of the wheel, removing the tire. I pinched my finger on the metal rim, but it wasn't serious. Still, I was so frustrated that I wanted nothing more than to start crying and lean against the tree, waiting for someone to rescue me.

This had to be the end of the trip for me. I'd never get back in time now. And I'd put so much of myself on the line. I grabbed the travel mug of lemonade and took a gulp. I stared at the tire that was lying on the ground, trying to remember how to patch the inner tube. I wondered if Miranda was going to drive past. I wondered if she had found the hundred dollars yet. Seeing the way she'd worked in the kitchen, she'd probably picked up and washed the plate while she was also putting away clean silverware.

A sink full of dishes. Soap bubbles! That was how Mason and Mr. Grant had taught me. I had to find the hole in the tube by making bubbles.

I traded out my travel mug for the water bottle and twisted off the mug's top, making a small bowl out of it. I filled it with water and separated the tube from the tire, first putting new air into it with my bike pump, and slid it into the water. I went around and around the tube, painstakingly pressing and looking for a bubble to appear.

It wasn't working. It didn't work. I was doing it wrong.

Then all of a sudden I had a bubble. I pushed the tube underwater and pressed. More bubbles.

I kept my finger on the hole with one hand and opened the patch kit with my other hand. I pulled out the small patch and container of glue. I used the corner of Stella's magic shirt to dry the tube section so the patch would stick. Then I used the tiny piece of sandpaper in the kit to rough up the area around the puncture. I squeezed glue onto the patch and pressed it firmly, holding it for two, then three, then five minutes, it seemed like. I wanted to get this right the first time around.

When I was confident it was set, I got my bike pump from my bike and inflated the tube. I held my breath as I waited to see if the patch had worked. I held the tire tube to my ear. I waited some more.

Then I slid the tube all the way inside the tire and attempted to put the tire back onto the rim with the little green tool. It took me about ten minutes, but I did it. I got the wheel back on the bike and closed the lever tightly.

After all that, I was almost afraid to look at my back tire. Thankfully, it was fine—if there was a new leak at all, it was a slow one. I brushed leaves, dirt, and pine needles off my shorts and legs and climbed onto the bike. Vowing to keep a closer eye on things, I headed back out onto the two-lane county road. My bike wobbled slightly. It felt like it was out of alignment. I'd probably damaged the tire rim when I crashed into the pothole. Maybe the sag wagon could fix that, if I ever found them again.

Traffic was picking up—probably some people were getting out of work—and I found myself wincing as each car sped by. I couldn't move over any farther or I'd run out of pavement.

I could see why riding with a group had advantages, even if it could be a little annoying at times to be in the back. As each car passed me, I felt more and more vulnerable about being on the road by myself.

I'd reached the end of the Frances Detour and had finally turned onto the road I needed to be on. According to Miranda, I'd have only a couple of miles on this road—a piece of cake. Blueberry cake.

I rounded a curve when suddenly two cars were coming toward me on the two-lane road. One was passing the other, and they were taking up the entire width of the road. The outside car flew past me, nearly running me off the road, and I realized all at once that this was exactly what had happened to Stella—a car coming this fast toward her. This fast, this out of control. Somebody texting, or somebody glancing away from the road, checking on a kid in the backseat or changing the radio station or just distracted about something and coming too close, crossing the center line.

The second car raced past me, and I felt its momentum threaten me, felt wind and hot exhaust on my legs, my ankles, through the small vents in my helmet even.

But I was lucky.

It missed me. As it whooshed by, I veered onto the shoulder as a cloud of road dust blew in my face, blinding me.

In that split second I knew what it might have felt like. How, in that short of a time, Stella's life was completely changed. I'd sensed it from the outside, but now I knew.

It wasn't fair.

It was so random.

Why her? Why not me?

I wasn't there with her. I was being stupid and trying on prom dresses for a prom we'd never go to now. I wasn't with her like I should have been.

I could have been riding on the outside of her. I could have blocked her, or maybe the car would have noticed us if we'd been two across instead of one.

Thinking about it made me start to shake and wobble and I fell over, landing awkwardly in a heap. I landed squarely on my left arm. My wrist was screaming with pain and felt like a hundred tendons had gotten torqued in the wrong direction. I got up slowly and gingerly touched my wrist. I didn't think I'd broken it, but I'd sprained it.

That was okay. I didn't need my wrist to ride, I said to myself as I picked up my bike. How many times did I have to get on and off it? This was getting—no, it was already beyond—ridiculous.

My wrist looked a bit awkward, so to support it I took off the magic shirt and made a bandage for it, wrapping the stretchy fabric around it and knotting it through the thumb and pinky finger.

That was when I heard a derailleur clicking. Out of the corner of my eye I saw someone coasting up to me. I couldn't believe my luck—to run into someone out here, this late in the day—

"Hey! Frances! Are you okay?"

It was Margo.

I didn't want her help. I didn't want anyone's. I didn't even deserve it. "I'm—well, I'm not great," I admitted.

"Did you take a shortcut?" Margo asked.

"No," I said. "I got lost, but I'm pretty sure I rode just as far—if not farther—than you."

"How come none of us have seen you since lunch?" she asked.

"It's a long story," I said. "The details aren't important."

"Your skin is really red," she said. "And did you hurt your wrist or something?"

My wrist was killing me, and I had no idea how I'd finish without a ride from the sag wagon. I could ask Margo to call Heather to come get me—I could probably ask her to call an ambulance, about my wrist.

But I wasn't doing that today. I'd made it this far. I was going to finish.

Don't. Just don't. Don't ask her for help.

"Are you okay? Do you have enough water?"

I got on the bike, gritting my teeth not to cry out as I lightly held the handlebars. "I'm not sure why you're asking," I said, as I started to ride. She clicked in right beside me. "I'm on my own from here on out. Isn't that right?"

"No. No, it's not."

We rode beside each other for a few minutes.

"You know, I wasn't just passing by, or doing extra miles. I came *looking* for you," Margo said.

I kept riding, eyes focused on the pavement ahead of me and the traffic beside me. My vision was a bit blurred as I stared at the white line of the breakdown lane. I wouldn't let her kindness get to me, not now. After everything I'd been through, there was a little crack in my resolve to be tough, to keep pushing through. The nicer she was to me, the more it widened.

"We were all worried about you," she said.

"Maybe you should get going," I said. "I know how it kills you to ride this slowly." I didn't want her around. I didn't want her to be nice to me. I was holding myself together with my anger toward her; if it was gone, I might fall apart.

She didn't say anything. She wasn't passing me, though.

We must have gone ten miles like that, not talking. When I saw the college with the Welcome, Cyclists! banner, I almost started crying. I'd made it.

Despite everything, I'd made it.

I wobbled toward the finish line, using my last ounce of energy to push the pedals those final few yards onto the campus. I stared down at my legs as I forced myself through. Everything about my body was in pain, but it was secondary to the way I felt inside. The reality of things was getting through. My gut ached, my chest was tight. I got off the bike, holding my wrist carefully.

Please nobody talk to me, I thought. *Please let me go off by myself and deal with this on my own.*

But no, for once my entire team was waiting for me, standing around the finish line. Apparently they'd sent Margo out as a scout or something, and they were all waiting for us to come back together. Cameron and Oxendale walked over and Cameron gave me a hand climbing off my bike, while Oxendale held the handlebars.

"You okay?" asked Elsa, coming closer.

"We've been worried sick!" Autumn cried. She held out a handful of orange slices. "Take one. Oh, your sunburn. It looks painful."

Unfortunately, Heather spotted us and marched over to me right away. "Frances, what happened to you? I nearly had to call your parents."

"I know I went off course. I can explain," I said. "Just give me a minute."

"Do you know how bad that is?" Heather wasn't about to let it rest. "It's like you think the rules aren't meant for you, but I'm sorry, they apply to everybody."

"I know that," I said. "Can you give me some time to wash up before you yell at me any more? I've had a pretty horrible day."

"You may have, and I'm sorry if you did. But not staying with the group—it has consequences," Heather said.

"I wasn't trying to leave the group," I said, feeling a rush of anger. "I'm here doing this ride, and the reason I'm doing it is because of Stella. Who was supposed to be here with me. Who would never have let me get lost. This isn't right. None of this is right."

"I—I'm sorry, Frances. It's a shame she isn't here, I agree," Heather said. "If only she hadn't broken her leg—"

"No," I interrupted Heather.

"No what?" she asked.

"No, she didn't break it," I said.

"What?"

"She lost it," I said. "Her leg got destroyed."

My whole body was shaking. I'd promised Stella I wouldn't tell anyone until the ride was long over, until she was ready to tell people herself. Now here I was blurting it in front of Heather, and Margo, and Cameron, and everyone.

"What—what are you saying?" asked Margo.

"They had to take off her leg. She lost her leg," I said, feeling the sickness rush up my throat when I remembered the scene, exactly as it had happened. Not the first day I saw her, but the second, when I'd stayed strong for her but fell apart as soon as I left the room.

I shoved my bike at Oxendale and ran away, as far and as fast as I could.

CHAPTER 14

When I'd gotten off the elevator to visit Stella, bringing breakfast and another bag with her stuff from home, one of the nurses I'd met the day before, when Stella was moved from the ER, had been sitting at the third-floor nurse's desk.

"Good morning." She smiled at me. "Don't take this the wrong way, but your outfits are improving," she said.

"Thanks. I guess," I said, moving closer to the desk. One nice thing about a small town is that the hospital isn't that big, either. You can get to know people if you want to. "So how's Stella doing today?"

"Mm," she hummed. "She's hanging in there. I'm sure your visit will make her feel better."

The way she didn't want to discuss Stella made me nervous. I looked at her name tag. "LaDonna? That sounds bad. Is it bad?"

"Sounds like nothing. Sounds like I have a lot of patients to keep track of and she's one of them," LaDonna said matter-of-factly.

"Got it," I said with a nod. "Thanks."

"Buzz us if you need anything," she said. "I'll be right in."

I walked down the hall toward her room, bracing myself but feeling mostly positive. I couldn't wait to deliver the things I'd brought: some from Stella's house, some from mine, and her favorite treats from Dunkin' Donuts. Even if she was on a restricted diet, I figured she could sip an iced latte through a straw.

"Franny, Franny! Wait."

I turned around and saw Stella's mom hurrying after me.

"Sorry, I was in the restroom." She coughed. "I'm glad you're here. Thanks for getting some more things for her."

"No problem," I said cheerfully, almost giving her a hug but then stopping. She wouldn't like that. She was too tough for hugs.

"I have to warn you, though," said Mrs. Grant. "She's in rough shape. She's . . . not doing very well. The damage to her pelvis and her leg—it's substantial."

I didn't understand what she was driving at. "Did she get worse overnight?" I asked.

I knew that could happen, but I assumed it only did so with older people. That had happened with my grandmother. She went from the flu to pneumonia to worse in what seemed like twenty-four hours before she passed away.

"I just—I want you to be aware that she's no longer in shock. Which means she knows more about what's going on, and she's a little bit worse than she was yesterday."

"Oh, I . . . sure. Okay." I'd dealt with Stella's extreme moods before. I could handle it.

Mrs. Grant must be overreacting, I thought. The whole family was a bit squeamish, to be honest. All except Stella.

"Why don't you and I go in together?" she suggested.

"Actually, if it's okay, I'll go in by myself."

"Oh, well. Are you sure?"

"Of course I'm sure. I'll, um, come get you if I need you," I said.

"I'll be right over there." She pointed to a hideous teal couch. Hospitals are full of bright, cheery colors, but as far as I'm concerned they should always be gray, to match the mood. Unless it's the baby center.

I walked into Stella's room, glad to be on my own so Stella and I could really talk. Her mom meant well, but she had a tendency to hover. We didn't always speak our minds when she was around. When we did, she'd often say, "Girls . . ." in this annoyed tone.

Stella was in bed, under the covers, the top part of it at a slight incline. She was reading on her tablet with her back turned to the door, and when she looked over her shoulder at me, she looked so much better that I was relieved. Sure, her face was a little puffy—but she wasn't as pale. Her straight dark-brown hair somehow wasn't straight anymore, as if they'd given her a bad haircut and left weird curls framing her face in the front. She didn't do curls. I did.

I set down the iced latte on her bedside table and pulled out a couple of doughnuts. "Glazed or maple?"

"I'm not hungry."

"Okay, maybe later," I said, resisting the urge to have one myself. I set the bag on a chair and tried to give her a hug, but she didn't budge. I patted her shoulder. She stared at me as if I were a stranger. "So what are you reading?"

"Just some dumb celebrity gossip," she said. "Nothing important."

"Let me see," I said, reaching for her tablet. "Who is it? What did Amanda Bynes do now? Or wait. Justin Bieber— please tell me he's dating a Jenner?"

"No!" she said, shoving the tablet under the covers. That

was weird, because we always looked at pathetic celebrity sites together, but whatever. She was feeling sensitive.

I opened the bag I'd brought and pulled out her oldest, still-living-with-some-fur stuffed animal, Cheeto, an orange tiger that had been hugged so much it hardly had any fur left. Stella kept Cheeto hidden on a top shelf in her closet, and I was pretty sure I was the only one who knew she still had him. Cheeto had seen us through a lot of agonizing moments when we were little. Flu shots. A wiggly tooth that had to be yanked out. The part in the first Harry Potter movie when Voldemort is drinking the blood of the unicorn.

"I don't need Cheeto," she said as soon as she saw him.

"Maybe not, but Cheeto needs you." I tossed the beloved, ragged tiger onto her bed.

She didn't pick him up. She didn't fix his torn ear so that it stood up right, the way she always did. She didn't even touch him.

"Come on, cheer up. I know this is terrible and horrible, but you'll get better quickly," I said.

"No. I won't," she said.

"I know it feels like that now." I started to push the bed rail down so that I could sit beside her. "But—"

"Don't," she said.

"I'm just going to sit down," I said.

She pulled herself up and wrestled with my arms a bit, trying to push me away. The sheets slipped, and that was when I realized it. Her legs weren't the same lengths. The leg closest to me, her left leg, was short. Below the knee, it was gone. Maybe the knee was even gone.

I quit wrestling, let go of the bedrails, and stood up, taking a step back, unable and unwilling to understand what was going on.

"Yesterday I was glad just to be alive. I didn't even know what happened, not really. This morning . . . I had surgery. It's real." Stella pulled the sheets and blanket more tightly around her.

"I'm sorry," I said. "Stells . . ."

"You can't tell anyone about this," she said. "Not anyone."

"What are you saying? You can't keep it a secret," I said.

"Why not?"

"You just can't! Your family is going to have to explain it when you miss school and—"

"It's *going* to be a secret. So do you think you could just *not* tell everyone for a while? God." She angrily threw Cheeto across the room, where he bounced off the window and landed on top of the window ledge, perched as if he were enjoying the parking lot view.

I walked over and stood beside the stuffed animal,

pretending to gaze out the window with him, blinking away hot tears.

"Do you want to know what I was looking at?" Stella said bitterly. "I was Googling how long it takes to get a new leg. Okay? I was reading about how my life is going to suck for the next six months. No, wait. For the rest of my life."

"No, it won't," I said, turning back to her. "We're going to make it work."

She didn't say anything in response. She was staring at the TV on the wall opposite her. It was an old *Simpsons* episode.

"How about the Cure Ride? How are we going to make *that* work?" she said. "Should I ride in the support van?"

"No, I'll do the ride for both of us," I said. "I'll get serious about it and raise money, and I can—"

"Why would you do that?" she said. "You hate cycling. That's why you weren't there."

She didn't say it, but my mind leaped to what she was thinking: *It could have been you. Maybe it should have been you. You don't even care about it, and I do.*

"I'm sorry," I said again, turning to face her, the tears now falling onto my shirt.

"And don't cry," she said. "God, Franny. *You're* fine. You're awesome. Just—"

"Stop it!" I said. "I'm crying because I hate that this

happened to you, not for me!"

"Yeah, well." Stella stared at the TV. "Life sucks, and then you die."

I went closer, but she refused to make eye contact. I stood there like a dolt for a few minutes, waiting for her to talk to me, to look at me. But she wouldn't.

"Stells. Please," I said. "Don't—don't give up."

"Shouldn't you be in school?"

"I don't have to—"

"I want to be alone. Don't you get it?" she snapped. "Just *leave* already."

Tears flooded my eyes, and I ran out into the hallway. Nurse LaDonna was walking past and grabbed me by the elbow. "You okay? You don't look like yourself," LaDonna commented, scrutinizing me. "You feeling all right?" She took my arm and guided me to a straight-back vinyl chair at the nurses' station. "Humor me and sit here for a minute. I'm going to get you something."

She went somewhere and I sat there, taking deep breaths, while my heart seemed to beat out of control.

"Have a cup of herbal tea." LaDonna held a tall stainless travel mug out to me. "Take it with you. You can keep the travel mug when you're done."

I eyed the tall mug. It was dark green, with white loopy

lettering that spelled out Mercy in a way that made it look like Merry. "Was this a Christmas thing?" I asked.

"What do you mean?" said LaDonna. "Now take a drink, get your bearings. This will help you." She turned to respond to a call from a patient's room. "I'll be right there," she said into the intercom, and then she marched off down the hall.

I took a small sip of the hot tea. I didn't even like tea that much, but it was weak and sugary and comforting. I studied the mug again, wondering if these were the mugs that got rejected. One time when I was on dance team we ordered these jackets that were supposed to say Shooting Sparks, but instead they said Shooing Spanks. We got replacements, but still, it was sad that nobody could use them. We were going to give them to Goodwill, but then we didn't want people walking around with the wrong message.

I got up and wandered out of the hospital, sipping the tea. I was too busy thinking about Stella to notice Mason coming through the revolving door until I stepped into the doorway before he had a chance to get out. Burning-hot tea splashed out the hole on top of the travel mug and landed on his shirt as we awkwardly rotated through the door to the sidewalk outside.

"Sorry," I said. "I—this mug. It's new."

"Or defective," said Mason as he brushed the drops off his arm onto his jeans.

"So. You were going in?" I asked.

"Yeah. I was here earlier, so I'm just coming back. Went to get some homework."

We stood outside the revolving doors. It was April, the time when the ground starts coming back to life, when mud turns into grass. The air smelled different, and birds were chirping. We both followed the sound and watched four sparrows chasing one another up to a slant in the roof, and the birds slipped underneath.

"That's why they call it Sparrowsdale, I guess," he said.

"Mason, I'm sorry," I said.

"Don't be sorry. She's going to be okay. It sucks, that's all, but she'll be all right," Mason said.

"I know. I know," I said, sounding like a chirping bird myself. "I'm going to do the ride anyway."

"I can help you get ready. If that's okay," Mason said. "It'll take my mind off . . . you know."

"No. I don't think it will," I said. We shared this look of recognition. Above us, the sparrows pecked and fought with one another, competing for space.

"Stupid birds," he said. "They could go anywhere."

CHAPTER 15

Cameron ran after me and grabbed

my arms when I stumbled on a rock, keeping me from falling. "It's okay. It's going to be okay," he said, but I couldn't stop shivering. My teeth were nearly chattering. It was the dumb bikini and my related sunburn. My skin was burning up and freezing cold at the same time.

"Come on, let's go talk to the group. I'm worried about you." Cameron guided me back to the finish area and we found a picnic table under the big food tent to sit down. The rest of our team quickly came over and gathered around me. "Autumn, grab her a Gatorade," Cameron said.

"And Alex—can you get some ice from the medical tent?" said Margo.

"It's— I need clothes. That's all," I said.

"That's not all," said Oxendale. "What's going on with your wrist?"

"I twisted it. But really, I just—I need some clothes," I said. "I'm freezing."

Within minutes Elsa had returned with a long-sleeved shirt and a fleece jacket for me; my wrist was resting on an ice pack; and I was sipping Gatorade fruit punch while Autumn sat across the table from me, looking concerned. Separate from Alex, for once. "They just started setting out dinner. What do you want? Take anything." Elsa set a plate of food in front of me.

Oxendale put one of his bike jerseys on my lap. "Sorry, it's all I've got, Franny."

"Please don't call me Franny," I said. I'd been wanting to tell him since Sunday, but for some reason I hadn't had the nerve until now. "Nobody calls me that except Stella and her family."

"Oh? Oh. Right," said Oxendale. "Sorry. You should have mentioned it."

"No, it's okay. I'm not trying to be a jerk. Really. Thanks for the bike-jersey blanket."

Max gave me a careful hug, his strong arms, his warm body making me feel safe. "Blondie, you don't look like yourself."

"Why didn't you tell us?" asked Margo. "No, wait. That's a stupid question. It wasn't up to you, was it? Stella decided."

I nodded. "She thought—I don't know. She just wanted more time to deal with it." I remembered her face, her panicked but cold face, that day at the hospital. How angry she'd been and how much I'd cried. "I wanted to do something. anything. So I thought it might make her feel better if I did the ride without her. But she hates the idea, deep down. I think she even hates me for knowing what happened to her," I explained.

Nobody said anything. Cameron was rubbing his calf, over and over, like he'd injured it earlier in the day. I wrapped my arms tightly around myself, still trying to warm up.

"I knew she was having a hard time, but I thought it was just, you know, her emotions," Cameron said.

"I thought she had facial injuries," Margo said.

"She did. She . . . does," I said.

"But this is so much more tragic," Autumn insisted. "I mean, scars heal. That's superficial. But losing a leg—"

"That's going to heal, too," I said fiercely.

"Right. I know. I know! That was stupid, what I said. Sorry," she apologized.

"No, it's not your fault. It's mine. I shouldn't have said anything." I wasn't okay with what I'd just done. I had promised to keep Stella's real situation a secret, and I'd kept it for weeks. Why was I breaking the promise now, with only three days left? "I promised Stella," I said. "She didn't want anyone to know, so I—I told her that I'd keep it a secret even though it was going to be impossible to pull it off. I was pulling it off, though."

"Kind of," said Margo. "But I had a feeling something else was going on besides a broken leg."

I turned to glare at her. She always had to compete. She always wanted to win. "Are you glad now? Because you were *right*?" I asked her.

"No," she said firmly, shaking her head. "I'm not *glad*. Do you really think that badly of me?"

I didn't say anything. Sometimes, yes.

"I wish I was wrong. I've been wishing I was wrong ever since I first started worrying about it." She was looking at me, her eyes shining intensely as if she were about to cry.

Suddenly I remembered her mother's illness. I had to stop being so insensitive. I wasn't the only one going through something bad—and it wasn't even me, it was Stella. I was just trying to support her. "I . . . no, I know you wouldn't want that," I admitted. "I'm sorry, Margo."

"It's okay. You're weak right now," she said.

There she went again with her helpful comments. Even in

trying to be nice and compassionate, she just couldn't commit to it. She had to slip in a dig of some sort.

"But she's so . . . so good," said Autumn. "It's not fair."

"It's not fair no matter how good she is," said Max. "I mean, a random accident like that . . ."

"That must have been hard. Did you talk about it with anyone?" Elsa asked. "Sorry. My mom's a grief counselor. It's the first thing she always asks."

"Not really," I said. "It helped being around other people who knew, even if we didn't talk about it. Like Mason. He's really the only one, except my mom. I couldn't talk about it too much with her, though, because she was freaking out about whether the same thing would happen to me. I thought she'd keep me from doing the trip, but I convinced her it'd be safe. And it felt safe. Until today when I was on my own."

"So, now we know. For better or worse," Margo said. "You can talk to us."

"You know, people do really well with artificial limbs," Alex said. "The advances they've made lately—the computers and mechanics—it's incredible. How about that guy who won gold medals in the Paralympics on artificial legs? Blade Runner?"

"And then he allegedly killed his girlfriend," Oxendale reminded us.

"Oh. Right. Well," Alex said, "I can't believe you brought that up." He frowned at Oxendale. "You have horrible taste sometimes, you know that?"

"I have an aunt who's in a wheelchair—she was in a motorcycle accident," Max said. "I know, big surprise, right? A family member who rides a Harley. Anyway, now she uses one of those hand-powered bikes? She's done marathons. This woman . . . she wasn't even someone who did sports before."

"That'll be Stella. For sure," said Oxendale.

"What if Stella doesn't want that?" I asked.

"Oh, she will. Please, it's Stella," said Margo.

I glared at her.

"Look, we may not be best friends, but we've competed with each other a lot over the years. Remember, I was on soccer, too—we did traveling team together for two years when I left dance. Plus this trip last year. And I'm not trying to make light of it or say it's all going to be peachy. You know that. You know I—well, I have experience with this kind of crap."

"Why, what happened to you?" asked Autumn.

"My mom. She's not well," said Margo.

"Is everyone going to spill something major tonight? If so, I'm going to have to get more marshmallows. Maybe a pack of cigarettes," joked Cameron.

"You smoke?" Max asked.

"I can't get over it," Autumn said. "Her whole life is flipped upside down because of one stupid accident and one stupid driver."

"She's lucky," Alex said. "She could have been killed, right? Any accident bad enough to lose a leg could have—"

"Can we not talk about it anymore?" I said.

"Sure, sure. Let's move on," Elsa said.

"So now we understand more of why you're doing this even after Stella dropped out. I mean, to be honest, it never made much sense to me," said Autumn, as she absentmindedly filed a stick to make it a good marshmallow roaster. "You weren't the type to put yourself out there. But now it all clicks."

The back of my neck prickled at her offhand comment. I wasn't the type of person who would put herself out there. Wherever "there" was. A place where outgoing super couples ruled the hallways and decided whether they'd talk to you based on some unpredictable formula? A place where you performed onstage until a better athlete and dancer told you that your look wasn't as uniform as the coach wanted it to be? *That* place?

I'd rather stay hidden, if those were my options.

"We know this has been torture for you," Alex added. He was talking in this sensitive-guy voice that made me want to bash him in the head. "I mean, you didn't do this last year, and there's a lot of stuff you can't plan for, unless you know. We could have been more helpful. Because we would never have been able to be a team without you." It was the first nice thing I'd ever heard him say. "So what can we do to help you?"

I sipped the fresh cup of ice-cold Gatorade Alex had brought me during one of the awkward silences, and ran one of the ice cubes across my shoulders to soothe my sunburn. I held the melting cube against my wrist, which was throbbing.

"There's something else," I added after a minute. "I have this list of things she wanted to do on this trip. I've been trying to complete it for her. Maybe you could help me with that after dinner?"

I took a short shower, then went to find Heather. We headed to the medical tent to get my wrist wrapped and some aloe and ointment for my sunburn. While I was there, Heather and I talked, and I gave her a blow-by-blow description of what had happened while I was lost. She seemed pleased by the decisions I'd made, and sympathetic as well.

Then I met the group at the outer ring of a large, but still sort of cozy campfire, which was part of the quiet, mellow evening that was planned for everyone. It was officially Campfire & S'mores night, and I was looking forward to having about a dozen.

Apparently we'd just gotten through the hardest part of the journey—the remaining three days were shorter lengths, more like forty-five to fifty miles instead of seventy, and we'd be heading back to the coast, where the terrain tended to be flatter. It wouldn't exactly be coasting from now on, but since there were four days down, and three to go, it felt like we'd really achieved something.

I wondered whether I should call Stella, but I felt like I'd left too many texts, too many unanswered messages. Maybe she was upset about me and Mason, though I had no idea how she'd know that anything had happened, unless he told her. He wouldn't have; I knew him.

I wondered if we should all call her, if we should just come right out and say, *Hey, everyone knows, and we all wanted to tell you we're riding for you now.* Then we could have a group hug. Over the phone.

She'd probably be furious. She wasn't a group hug person. And, I had to admit, neither was I.

I sat next to Cameron, by the side of the campfire where the flames were small but the coals were glowing red. Perfect for marshmallow roasting. The night was getting cool, and I shivered a little; with the sunburn I had, I was either too hot or too chilled.

While we passed around graham crackers and chocolate,

and waited for marshmallows to toast just right, I told everyone how Stella had planned the F-It List for herself. How
she'd joked about all her goals the past few months, and I
thought it was all in her head, that she was just trying to get
me psyched to do the ride. How I'd found the list sitting by
her laptop. It seemed important to her, but I hadn't known
that she was that deliberate about it.

"So, the surfer girl outfit today. Was that . . . ?" Cameron
asked.

"Yes, that was on the list—I'd never do something like
that, ever—and when she's better, I'll tell her how awful it
was," I said. "In detail."

"I think she'll see your sunburn lines and know," said
Margo.

"You're right." It would have been funny if my skin weren't
inflamed. I'd taken a mostly cold shower and applied gobs of
aloe to my shoulders, back, and neck.

I went through the other things on the list that I'd done:
the spur-of-the-moment dance party; leaving a giant tip at the
diner; dancing in the rain; getting my navel pierced.

I didn't mention the night I'd gotten slightly tipsy from
sharing a spiked lemonade. Nobody would want to hear about
me breaking another rule.

I also didn't mention the epic kiss with Mason. Which, now

that I thought about it, had been more like epic kisses, plural.

The more I thought about it, the more worried I was. Stella didn't need the extra aggravation of the two of us. Maybe I was reacting to the fact that I hadn't heard from Mason in twenty-four hours. Of course, I didn't have my phone, so . . . that was difficult.

"So the whole dancing-in-a-downpour thing. That wasn't your idea, either?" asked Cameron.

"Wait. I didn't see this," said Margo.

"No, it was a solo—I mean, private performance," I said. That sounded just as bad. "Cameron and I were caught in a thunderstorm—when we did the farm detour. That's all. That's why no one else was there."

"So there was the dance party *and* the rain dance," Oxendale said. "I didn't know Stella wanted to dance that much."

"Yeah, I guess I . . . I guess I didn't know that, either." I was the one who always danced and wished I could be athletic, like Stella; now I was finding out that she maybe wanted to be a little more like me. But now, for a while, she wouldn't be able to dance. At all.

"Closet dancer," said Max, nodding. "We'll put that on her permanent record."

"So there are a couple of things left to do," I said. "Start a food fight. Sleep under the stars."

"That shouldn't be too hard," said Cameron, gazing upward. "Tonight we're close to a city but tomorrow night we're not."

"No, that one should be easy. But worst of all, I have to do some insane ride at Phantom Park. It's the Devil's Drop of Doom. Have you guys heard of it? I'm going to freak out. I'm just telling you now. I don't like heights."

"So, I'll do it instead of you," Elsa said. "I tried it once last summer when it opened. It was fine."

"I can do it for you—for her—too," said Margo.

"But you guys can't . . . I mean, I have to do it," I said. "I'm the one who's doing the list."

"Frances, you can't do all this by yourself. I mean, look what it's done to you," said Cameron.

"What? I'm fine. Basically."

"Your wrist is screwed up. You're sunburned." Cameron counted off the various issues on his fingers. "You're exhausted from riding more than two hundred miles during the past four days—I mean, you're doing this with a lot less training than we've had."

"Which is all my own fault," I reminded him.

"*And* you're riding with the whole weight of worrying about Stella. *We* haven't had that. Not until now," Cameron added.

"I appreciate the offer, but I have to do it because—look, I just do," I said.

"We'll do it together, then. There's no law against that," said Margo. "The seats are two across. I went last summer. I'll go with you."

"I'll sit behind you and get it on video," Elsa said.

"I'll cheer?" said Autumn.

"I'll buy cotton candy or whatever you want after you're done," Alex said.

"I guess there's only one job left for us. That means the three of us have to catch her when she falls," Max joked to Cameron and Oxendale.

I pushed him in the chest. "Not funny."

I stared into the fire, watching the coals break apart. I felt so relieved to have the truth out in the open. I felt equally guilty, though.

I have to call Stella and be honest, I thought. *I have to tell her that I broke my promise to keep her real condition a secret.*

"Can I borrow someone's phone for a minute?" I asked.

"Sure, take mine," said Elsa.

I found a private spot and dialed the familiar number. For once, she answered.

"Hey, it's me. I borrowed Elsa's phone. How's it going?" I asked.

She cleared her throat. "My phone rang ten minutes ago and I thought it was you," she said. "But it was Margo."

"Why would she . . . call?" I asked, glancing across the campfire at Margo.

"She wanted to know how I was. She wanted to know how my *recovery* was going. Margo. Of all people."

"She's not awful," I said. "She probably genuinely wanted to know—"

"Why would she do that? I can't imagine why she'd be so concerned about me, unless of course . . . you told her."

Right. That was why I was calling her. To tell her the truth. "Listen, it wasn't something I wanted to do—"

"I can't believe you. You promised you wouldn't tell," she said angrily.

"I—I tried not to. I didn't do it deliberately, but—"

Click. She ended the call.

CHAPTER 16

As exhausted as I felt, I didn't get much sleep Wednesday night.

It was like once I began remembering that day, that horrible, upsetting day when Stella talked to me as if I were nothing and no one, as if I were the one who'd let it happen to her, I couldn't stop thinking about it.

How awful the accident must have been for Stella.

How downright gory. Nightmarish.

How it all happened in the blink of an eye.

I tossed and turned, each time wincing because my wrist would shift position or the sleeping bag would rub my sunburn the wrong way. Then there were the three times I had to get up in the middle of the night because I'd had so much water and Gatorade. My piercing was the least of my problems—I'd been cleaning it religiously, determined not to let it get infected. That happened when I finally got my ears pierced at thirteen, and it wasn't pretty.

Thursday morning's ride to Newburyport, in Massachusetts, was hilly, but nothing approaching the Mount Washington–style peaks of the day before. I had a brand-new tube in my front tire, and the rim had been straightened by one of the mechanics. I also got to wear comfy clothes again. And best of all, I always had someone from my team riding beside me, and every once in a while one of the riders in the front would ride back to check in on me, and switch places. I liked the variety, getting to hang out with someone different—although of course when it was Alex and Autumn, they'd had to both come back and ride with me, one on each side. That could be considered progress, though. At least they weren't *right* next to each other.

Just before lunch, around one, we reached the ocean. We stopped at a scenic overlook.

Stella loved the ocean. So much. I thought about the times in junior high we'd begged and begged our parents to take us to the beach and how they always insisted it was "too far," because they had to work, or we had to go visit someone, or my mom didn't want to get sand in the house because we were having people over. Now I'd gotten here on a bike—not all the way from home, but pretty close.

When I turned around from looking out at the water, our whole team was standing behind me. "You okay?" asked Cameron.

"Um, of course I'm okay," I said. I brushed past them and walked over to the large metal-and-stone sculpture of a boat that marked the spot as a memorial to a lost ship. The sign below a large boat said:

The John Q. Chambers Memorial Lobster Boat—
Wrecked in 1879 Near This Spot
Three Lives Were Lost as the Mighty Sea Raged

Surrounding the boat were bronzed sailors in hats, slickers, and boots, clinging to the sides. The sculpture looked a bit neglected, but still had freshly painted signs on it that said:

DO NOT CLIMB OR MOUNT!
PLEASE STAY OFF—THIS MEANS YOU!

Another sign was covered by graffiti: a face with googly eyes, a flourish of a nose, buck teeth, and a tongue sticking out.

As I walked around to check out the other side, a voice called from above me.

"Come on up!" said Max. I looked up and saw him sitting atop the boat. "Come on, guys. If we're going to break some rules, we've got to start somewhere."

I took a tentative step toward the sculpture. Cameron, Oxendale, and Margo scaled the small ship, while Elsa, Autumn, Alex, and I watched.

"Excuse me—A.J.? Would you mind taking our picture?" Max called to another rider standing nearby. "Autumn, you have your phone on you? Come on, everyone, crowd around. Let's all get in the shot. Frances, don't be last—come on, statues don't bite."

I stepped up between one of the sailors and the boat in a little toehold. One of the sailor's arms was broken off at the elbow. The feeling of the jagged edge made me shiver as I leaned against it; I hated rough surfaces.

Everyone was laughing and leaning in for the photo. This wasn't on the F-It List, but I still felt as though this was for Stella. I craned my neck forward and yelled, "Everyone say 'Stella,' okay? One, two, three, Stella!"

"*Stella!*" Max cried at the top of his lungs, imitating Marlon Brando from an old movie that Stella kind of hates because it makes everyone scream her name like that.

Just like that, everyone started yelling her name, louder and louder, making dramatic poses, flinging our arms out as if we were all onstage in *A Streetcar Named Desire*.

"Hey! You kids!" A gruff-sounding man was walking toward us. "Get down from there! Show a little respect!"

Our lunch stop was at a park on the water, and our bikes filled an entire parking lot, along with long tables covered with bag lunches. I grabbed one that said *Turkey/Swiss* and headed for a shady section in the dunes, where I wouldn't get more sun. I ate the way I'd been doing all week—quickly, downing my sandwich, chips, fruit, and a cookie in record time. I'd probably lost ten pounds on this trip already, just by exercising, not that I cared.

"Hey, Frances!" Cameron called to me as I was dropping things in the recycling bin. "Time to cross off something else."

"What are you talking about?" I asked with a laugh. "Did you have a food fight without me?"

"Never," said Max.

"Listen," Oxendale said. "Stella did say to ride in a bikini and swim in bike clothes, right?"

"Sure," I said slowly.

"Well? What are you waiting for? You think we'll get a

better chance than right now?" Oxendale threw out his arms. "There's the Atlantic, baby!" He started to take off his cycling jersey, and I cringed. I did not need to see Oxendale's skinny white belly.

"That's not on the list!" Margo called to him as I walked beside her toward the water's edge. "It's swim *in* your bike clothes."

I'd never been more grateful to her. "Thank you," I said, taking off my bike shoes before I stepped onto the sand.

"Oh, yeah, sure." She placed her shoes carefully under the boardwalk. "There's no way I'm taking off my clothes, either—and you know that would be the next thing they'd ask if they took off theirs."

I ran into the surf and almost got knocked out by the coldness of the water. I went out as far as I dared, closed my eyes, and dunked my head underwater. Then I dove all the way in, pushing off the sand with my feet, enjoying the rush of cold water surrounding my body. Swimming. It was another thing that Stella would have to adjust to. Swimming in the ocean. One of her favorite places, one of her favorite things. I stayed underwater, holding my breath, trying to imagine how that would feel.

My bike clothes were sopping wet as I strode out of the surf. We all looked a bit like drowned rats, to be honest.

Heather was standing on the shore, waiting for us. "I'm *pretty* sure that swimming after lunch wasn't on the itinerary."

"Nope," said Cameron.

She shrugged. "I guess I can count it as a triathlon move. It'll have to be okay. Come on, everyone's getting ready to go. I suddenly realized the Sparrowsdale team was missing. I had a feeling you'd be down here somewhere, but swimming? At this temperature?"

"Aw, the water's perfect," said Cameron. "You should try it. Come on."

"No, I couldn't," she said. "We have to get—"

"Come on," Cameron urged again. "It's just water. And it does feel surprisingly good."

"Why are you all doing this? I feel like there must be some ulterior motive, since you're the only group down here crazy enough to do this."

"It's for Stella," I said.

"Oh." She smiled at me. "Well, in that case. Somebody get *this* on video." Heather slipped off her flip-flops and dove in.

It might sound horrible, but none of us showered before dinner that night. We'd already gone swimming, and besides, we knew what was in store. I didn't have enough clean outfits left to spare, but I was hoping other people did—the idea wasn't for people to hate us, just to have fun. With only two nights left to this trip, now was the time.

"I absolutely love food fights," said Oxendale. "They're just brilliant."

"How can we have a decent food fight outdoors, though? Everyone can just run away."

"There are ways. And I bet other people have some steam to let off. If we get everyone in on it, then nobody will get in trouble—what are they going to do, kick us all off?" said Max.

"It's like you've done this before," Autumn said. "Were you behind that horrible shepherd's pie incident sophomore year? Oh my gosh. That *was* you."

Max grinned, leaning back with his hands behind his head.

"I have a suede jacket that still smells like ground beef and corn after three cleanings. It's disgusting," said Autumn. "You should have to buy me a new one."

"I accept no responsibility for that," said Max. "In fact it's pretty much my life goal to not take responsibility for much. Except this ride. This thing matters to me."

"Me too," said Oxendale.

On a signal from Max, who was watching Heather and

the other adults' table to make sure they weren't paying attention, I launched a grape tomato with my spoon, sending it flying through the air, across our picnic table, the next one, and then bouncing off a girl's head at the next table.

She rubbed her head and looked around, but didn't seem to think anything of it.

I had to up my game.

I'd loaded my plate with items from the salad containers: baby carrots, cucumber slices, grape tomatoes, purple onion, and best of all, cottage cheese.

I took a glob of the cottage cheese and slung it across the table, over Max's shoulder, square on the boy sitting behind him.

As soon as it landed on his back, he jumped up. "What the—"

That's when Margo flung a forkful of pasta—with tomato sauce—in the air, just as Max pitched a handful of spaghetti, Oxendale tossed two meatballs, rapid-fire, and Autumn lobbed a dinner roll across three tables.

"Food fight!" somebody yelled—even before I had a chance to say it.

"Food fight!" everyone started screaming, or else they were screaming from being smacked in the face with pasta, salad, or maybe pasta salad.

I emptied my plate, tossing things in every direction, while being pelted with all the same foods. I couldn't stop laughing as I fired carrots into the air like little missiles. A shower of food was literally falling from the sky, while Heather and the other people in charge hid under their table, grabbing the megaphone now and then to call for us to stop.

When it was finally, mercifully over, I wiped apple pie and whipped cream and a baby carrot off my face, pulled spaghetti out of my hair, and peeled the cucumber slice off my arm, where it was stuck with ranch salad dressing that was acting like glue.

"You—you—have—" Cameron was pointing at me and stammering, laughing so hard he couldn't get the words out.

"What?" I said, and the more he laughed, the more I couldn't stop laughing, either. My stomach hurt, I was laughing so hard, and when I bent over in pain, something slid off my head onto the ground.

"You have—you had—a brownie on your head," he finally said. "Can I have it?"

We both lunged for the brownie at the same time, bumping into each other. We collapsed on the ground, still laughing, rolling in cottage cheese and spaghetti sauce and who knew what else. Like we would even eat that brownie or anything that had been thrown by someone else. Of course, what *were* we going to eat now?

"Jell-O wrestling? Get a room," Autumn said.

"We don't *need* a room!" I shouted at her. Then I turned to Cameron. "God. The two of them. They're so clueless sometimes. It's like they only recognize people as parts of couples, like it's the only way to be."

"That's because they haven't been apart since—since—the invention of stuffed pizza crust," he said.

"You know when that *was*?" I asked.

"Sure, it was when Autumn and Alex saw each other across seventh-grade homeroom and fell madly in love," Cameron said.

"This is too fun," I said. I started to cry, the salt running down my face and mixing with my sweat-salt, all Salt Lake City on me.

"Too fun? That's a thing?" Cameron asked, wiping a green glob off his neck and shivering when he looked at it. "No, you're right. This is sad. Someone just wasted an avocado." He held it out to show me, but I wouldn't look at him. I couldn't. I was still crying a little bit.

"You have whipped cream on your eyebrows," he said.

"Yeah, well." I looked up from under the tangle of curls that was my hair at the moment. "You have a spaghetti-sauce Mohawk."

"If I could get the meatballs and make them earrings, this would be a look," he said.

I laughed, despite myself. "A crazy look. A look that would make people never sit next to you on the bus."

"People never do sit next to me. That's why I ride my bike. You dig?"

"No," I said. "And that's not true. You're totally popular. You have plenty of friends."

"Sure, but not on our bus route," he said, laughing.

We both stood up and started hunting for some paper towels, napkins, anything we could use to wash up with. People were starting to clean up, using plastic gloves and trash cans. The gloves seemed pointless considering we were all mostly covered in food, anyway.

"But you know what? Despite the royal couple being on this trip, and Margo lecturing us right and left—it's been fun. I didn't really know you before. Now I've, like, bared my soul to you, and meanwhile, you've hated being here—"

"No, I haven't," I said. "Only—the first day. Maybe the second. But you—you were the one who made it okay. I'm really grateful."

"The grateful speech? Please, no," he said. "We've already been over this. We're not in the same sector, and it wouldn't work out." He smiled at me. "I do know one thing for sure."

"What?" I was kind of dreading his answer.

"I don't think we can sleep under the stars tonight."

"No? Why?"

"All this food on the ground. It's going to attract a whole lot of raccoons, squirrels, mice. . . ." His phone rang and he slipped it out of his pocket, then stepped aside to answer. After a minute he handed the phone to me. "Some guy named Mason wants to talk to you. Wait—is he the one who almost got us kicked off the trip?"

"It wasn't his fault," I said. "It was mine." I took the phone and wandered off to get a little bit of privacy. "Hey."

"Hey, you okay?"

"Uh. Mostly."

"You're almost done. I was thinking maybe Stella and I could come see you at the finish. Would that be okay?" asked Mason.

"With me? Sure. Okay with Stella? No." I shook my head. "Probably not."

"Why not?"

"She hates me."

"She does not."

"Trust me. She does. I cracked under pressure last night. I got lost, I got a flat tire, I was run off the road by a car, and I started feeling really guilty for not being there with

Stella. And then everyone was mad at me and telling me how I shouldn't be on the ride and I just—I needed to tell them. I needed to talk about it with someone other than the inside of my brain."

"So . . . how did they react?" Mason asked. "Were they shocked?"

"They were really upset. They felt kind of blindsided. But . . . it was a good thing, I think. People had been wondering why they hadn't seen her and what was going on. They really care about her. And people want to help, you know?"

"Sounds positive," said Mason. "I guess."

"Right. But then Margo had the idea to call Stella and be extra sympathetic, and immediately Stella knew that I'd spilled. When I called, she hung up on me."

"Oh. Not good."

"Right. I told her I only did it because I—I couldn't keep it to myself anymore. The pressure and the lies and—people are going to find out. She can't hide forever."

"She just wanted you to buy her some more time. She's doing better, I promise," Mason said, sounding upbeat. "This therapist she's been meeting with has been helping her a lot."

"Enough that she'll come to see us at the finish?" I asked.

"Sure. Why not?"

"Because she's stubborn and she's mad at me," I reminded him.

"Maybe you don't understand her as well as you think you do," said Mason.

"What's that supposed to mean?"

"Half the time she's mad at me, and I don't even do anything. You've just been spared that side of her until now."

"Mason . . . this is a little more serious than dumb sibling fights," I said. "It's okay if she's mad at me because I'm in the world and she's mad at the world."

"I think I know what you're saying. Granted, this is like way outside anything we've ever experienced. But I'll ask her again." Mason sighed. "I can't guarantee anything. But I'll mention I talked to you."

"Have you . . . you know," I stammered. "Or are you going to . . . mention anything else? About us?"

"Like what?"

He sounded completely clueless, like our night together wasn't on his radar at all. "The fact that you and I . . . you know," I insisted.

"No, I really don't. You and I what?" he asked in a teasing voice. "Tell me about it. Especially the good parts."

"Mason." I felt my face getting hot. I remembered the way he'd touched my face, how it felt to be close to him.

"Anything good? Refresh my memory," he said. "Did it have something to do with your navel, or did I dream that part?"

I laughed. Maybe I didn't have to worry about whether we'd only had a one-night thing.

CHAPTER 17

Friday night we camped near Marblehead and had a big celebration, with Heather going over everything we'd accomplished and giving out awards for dollars raised, sprints won. Our team had gotten more contributions as the days went along, and I learned there had been a recent hundred-dollar gift made specifically with my name on it. When I pressed the woman in charge of finances for details, she said it was made by a donor who wanted to be listed as anonymous, but there was a message attached to it: "Frances, if you ever feel lost again, you know where to find me—Miranda."

She'd taken the hundred dollars I'd given her and turned it into a contribution to the cause.

As a reward for being nearly done, and for raising so much money, Phantom Park gave our whole group free admission for the night and unlimited rides.

That was the part I was dreading. I'd been hoping that they'd canceled their offer, or that it would pour rain, or lightning would force them to close the park. No such luck.

I wanted *limited* rides. Carousels and bumper cars. The things that stayed on the ground.

We walked in groups to the amusement park, about a mile away. As we got closer, I saw the lighted outlines of roller coasters as they raced up and down, the Ferris wheel spinning slowly in the night sky.

Then I saw the Devil's Drop of Doom.

Cameron and I had checked out some YouTube videos of the ride so I could get a better idea of what I was in for. The problem was, I couldn't watch the videos without feeling dizzy.

There was a gleaming red "devil" train (complete with fire images and horns) that went up. And up. And up.

When it reached the top, the train leveled off briefly and paused for a second.

Then it barreled straight down toward the ground at a hundred miles an hour.

Until the bottom, when it once again leveled out and

pulled up to the Ride End sign.

I'd watched videos of people screaming, laughing, and shouting on the ride. But I could not imagine myself on that train, for the life of me.

It was going to be like one of those breathtaking death drops you see at airshows, when you think the plane might be about to crash, only it's pulled up at the last second by a daredevil pilot. Usually. And everyone oohs and aahs and admires the thrill. Everyone except me, because I can't even *watch* that kind of thing.

Any positive energy I'd felt from being surrounded by my team was starting to disappear. The last hundred yards of walking into the park, getting wristbands, and finding which way to go seemed to take hours instead of minutes.

Stella no doubt wanted to do this ride because she loved adventure. She was brave and fearless. Up until now, next to her I'd been her wimpy sidekick. I didn't do the hard stuff.

As we stood in the long line, I listened to people screaming on the ride. I closed my eyes, not wanting to watch. That made me queasy, so I opened them and started reading all the warning signs that were posted along the line. They weren't exactly reassuring. I didn't want to experience zero gravity. The line was moving forward—too quickly.

"I'm sorry," I said to Margo, who was beside me, "but I can't."

"You can do it," she said. "You'll be fine."

"Okay, then. I *won't*," I said.

"You will," she said. "Don't think about what bothers you. Think about how cool it's going to be when you're done."

"It'll be over before you know it," said Cameron, standing behind me. "And we're all going to sit with you, so it's not like you're going to fall out."

I shook my head back and forth. "I can't, I can't!"

"Yes, you can," said Margo. "Take a few deep breaths. Nothing bad is going to happen. This place has an A-plus-plus safety rating."

"I'm not worried about that," I said. "I'm worried I'll freak."

"Hate to tell you this," said Autumn, "but you're already freaking out. So you can quit worrying about it. Try to relax."

RELAX?! I almost shouted. This ride was about to crush me. Not literally, of course, just . . . psychologically. I'd be a babbling idiot who'd need to be carted away to the hospital if and when I ever got the strength to buckle up in one of the seats.

A minute later Max was pushing his way through the line behind us. "Look who I found," he said.

"Frances!" Scully cried. "Long time no see. Where've you been?"

"Oh . . . pretty much everywhere," I said.

"Thought you could use some moral support," Max said in my ear.

Margo and Autumn looked at me, and then at each other.

"How do you . . . know him?" asked Elsa.

"Oh, I've met a lot of people on this trip. You have no idea." I stepped aside with Scully, ducking under the back half of the awning where ride cars would pull up. Scully had a bike bottle in his hand, and I had a feeling I knew what was inside it.

"Max said you need some liquid courage. So come on, take a sip. It'll help." He passed me the bottle.

I held it in my hand a few seconds. It was tempting. I could crush my fear with a few slugs of this stuff, if I wanted to. Actually, I didn't know if it would work that way at all. It could be the opposite. "Thanks, but no, I don't think so. I mean . . . I could get sick on the ride. I'm keeping my food and bevs to a minimum."

"Come on. You don't even have to do this ride. We're going to check out the castle soon. Remember? We can hang out in the mansion, sipping cocktails?"

"I can't. I have to do this. And I think this is something I have to get the guts for on my own," I said, "or else it won't count." I handed the bottle back to him. "Thanks, though."

"If you don't have a sip, then I will," said Scully. "Would that help?" He smiled.

"Sure. You do that. I'll live vicariously. You're cool with that, right?"

"Be my guest. See you on the flip side. Literally."

My stomach lurched a bit as I found Margo in line. We were near the front now. In fact, people were getting out of the car that we were supposed to get into.

"I used to be afraid of these kinds of rides too," Margo said as we waited for it to pull up beside us. "Then I figured out how not to be scared. You have to get mad."

The car stopped in front of us. It seated eight, and we were eight. Margo gently pushed me into the front row. "Mad at what? Oh my God, oh my God. I can't get onto this."

"You're on it," said Margo. "Accept it. Sit down."

I took short, panicky breaths as I fastened the safety belts around my shoulders, my waist.

"What are you mad at right now?" asked Margo. "Besides me for making you do this and for all the other things you're mad at me about. Besides this ride, because I know you hate this, I know you hate heights, and you probably are going to hate the person running the ride."

There was a loud *ka-chunk* sound as bars lowered in front of us. "Is there a panic button?" I asked, looking over my shoulder. "So they can stop the ride?"

"No. Once it starts—look, once it starts, it's practically over. The anticipation is the worst part."

My palms were sweating. I felt my stomach churn. I'd rather have died. Almost.

"So come on," Margo urged. "What are you mad at?"

Myself, for being such a wimp, I thought.

"Talk to me."

I'm mad because I'm here. I'm mad at what happened to Stella, and I'm mad at Stella because it's been weeks now and I've been doing this ride as well as her F-It List, which includes things that terrify me. I'm doing it all for Stella, and Stella won't even talk to me long enough for me to tell her what I'm up to and why.

The ride started moving and I gripped my seat, and then Margo's hand as we shot forward.

But more than that, I was angry because a split second changed everything.

I didn't know that was a thing, not really, before now.

Now I would have to live knowing that everything could be gone in a second. I didn't want to think like that. I was only just figuring how to do this thing that was life.

We went up. And up. And up.

"If you don't want to talk, let out a primal scream!" Margo yelled to me as we ascended the towering track.

We were at the top all of a sudden. The moment I dreaded more than anything. The train stopped and I looked out at the horizon, at the ocean in the distance, at our little blue tent city in a clearing, at all the people milling around below us.

Then there was another *ka-chunk!* and we plummeted.

I screamed. Like I'd never screamed in my life. My hair went straight up, and Margo's whipped me in the face as we zoomed to the ground. "Pull up!" I yelled. "Pull *up!*"

Afterward, I borrowed Margo's phone and called Stella. I didn't want to tell her about the ride or the stars or the list or anything else. I needed to tell her something else.

"Please, promise me you'll come tomorrow," I said, "to the finish. Mason will drive you. Please?"

"I don't know. I don't think I'm ready," she said. "Besides. You *told* people."

"I broke down, okay? I'm not you," I said. "I'm not strong."

She was quiet for a minute. "Yes, you are," she said.

"Sorry, this isn't about me. I got sidetracked. Please try to come," I said. "Everyone really wants to see you. And since, unfortunately, they do know what really happened to you,

you have no reason to hide anymore. I mean, I'd think it'd be freeing, in a way."

"Well, it's not," said Stella, "in another way. Sorry, but I have to go."

"Okay, but before you do—look, there's something I have to say. You can't hold it against me anymore."

"What?"

"The accident. It wasn't my fault."

"I never said it was," Stella replied.

"But I *feel* like it was. It was a horrible, awful, tragic thing, and I'm sorry I wasn't there. I'm sorry I was at Flanberger's trying on stupid dresses, instead of riding with you like I should have been," I said. "Maybe I could have gotten hit instead of you, or maybe we wouldn't have been at that curve at that time because I'd have slowed you down. But I wasn't there. I'll be sorry about it for as long as you want me to be, but I can't change what happened."

She didn't respond for a few seconds. Then she said, "Neither can I."

Later that night, instead of climbing into our tents as usual, we quietly took them down, leaving our sleeping bags and everything else about us open to the sky, and to the rest of the riders. Luckily, it was a clear night, with a half-moon—there were plenty of stars to see.

"Why aren't you guys using your tent?" asked a girl next to us, coming back with her toothbrush.

"We're just not, tonight. We want the fresh air," I said.

"We want to sleep under the stars," added Margo. "Just once on this trip, you know?"

"Okay. Maybe we won't keep our tent up, either," the girl said.

I wasn't sure who was passing the word around but slowly, gradually, tents across the field went down, rolled up and set aside, almost like a coordinated display at a football game. I stood up and looked and almost every tent was down, and the field was filled with people just sitting on sleeping bags, talking, or lying down and gazing upward. I didn't know if this was what Stella wanted, but it was an incredible feeling of community, of the power of all of us to do one important thing. Like this ride.

"Pass the bug spray," said Margo.

"Did you have to ruin the moment?" I asked.

"I didn't know we were having a moment," she said.

"Well, yeah. Isn't this cool? I mean, look. *All* these people are doing Stella's F-It List now. Can anyone get a video of this?" I asked.

"I'll do it," said Elsa softly.

"Or you could." Max held out a phone to me. As I took it from him, I felt the familiar rubber case, the grooves in the checkered pattern.

My phone! "Where was it?"

"It was in the bottom of the tent bag. It must have gotten wrapped up in the tent," Max said. "There's this little flap of fabric at the bottom of the tent sleeve, and it was underneath that. I'm sure it's dead, but . . ."

"No, this is wonderful. Thank you!" I leaned forward and kissed him on the cheek.

"Oh, uh, sure." Max's face turned beet red. For someone who always acted a little bit older and more knowing than the rest of us, Max suddenly looked like an embarrassed eighth grader.

Max was right. The phone was dead. I tucked it into my pocket. Then I climbed up onto a rock beside Elsa and we both looked down at the sea of people sleeping under the stars as she recorded a few minutes' worth of footage.

This was it. The end of the list. The end of this impossibly long journey. But maybe the beginning of another one.

CHAPTER 18

Saturday morning, we all took off
our ride name and number bibs and turned them over to the
blank side. Then, using a Sharpie, we wrote Stella's name, letter by letter, so when we rode in a line we spelled her name.
Autumn drew a giant red heart on her race bib, while Elsa
put an exclamation point on hers, which was ironic, since she
hardly ever said anything above a whisper.

We rode together all morning, staying eight across whenever we could, spelling out different words when we got
bored: LATE. SEAT. SLATE. LAST. We were a moving
Boggle game.

The roads got busier and narrower as we reached the city,
all three hundred eighty-plus of us. They'd closed a couple of

streets to traffic as we neared the finish line, right in the heart of Boston at Faneuil Hall—one of the oldest marketplaces in the city.

The plan was for the entire group to finish all together, in a show of solidarity. I'd never ridden in such a huge bunch before, and I had to admit that it felt pretty cool to be one of the pack.

There were people holding signs, cheering for us, applauding in appreciation. They couldn't all be family members or friends . . . so were these just random people? Everyone was so enthusiastic for us. I felt like I might start crying. I glanced over at Elsa, the exclamation point to my *A*, and she already was.

When she caught me looking at her, she said "Allergies," and brushed the moisture off her face.

"Elsa? You keep saying that," I said. "But I'm worried about you. What's going on?" She never gave out any details about what was going on with her, and since our paths rarely crossed at school, I really didn't know.

"Nothing," she said.

"But it's not allergies, is it?" I asked.

"No." She shook her head. "I cry when I'm happy," she said. "And riding makes me happy. My mom keeps telling me I have to express myself, so I do it while I'm riding, when nobody sees. Which also makes me happy." She laughed. "I'm pretty sure my mom spends too much time reading books about grief."

Margo and Max urged us to ride faster when we saw the One Mile Left sign, so we picked up the pace. I couldn't believe there was only one mile to go, out of three hundred fifty. I'd never have made it without this team, without Mason helping me train, without the F-It List to keep me focused on something other than the pain in my legs every day from riding.

Half mile left!" Cameron yelled, and we pumped even harder, sprinting, all the time being encouraged and cheered for like we were Olympians instead of some high school students from northern New Hampshire.

I hoped Stella was here to see our shirts. We had to weave around a few slower riders to stick together, eight across. She'd probably be embarrassed, but secretly she would love it.

We cleared the finish line to a chorus of shouts of "Go Stella!" and I figured everyone thought she was suffering from childhood cancer, and I felt bad if we were misleading them on that.

We coasted to a stop on the plaza and climbed off our bikes. I searched the crowd frantically for Stella and Mason. The place was too mobbed to see anyone, really. Mason and I had agreed to meet by the Sparrowsdale pickup spot, and each team had a little sign tied to a chair where they should meet up. Our bags and other gear had already been dropped and were waiting for us there.

I knew it would take a few minutes for Mason and Stella to make their way over to us—if she wasn't feeling well, she'd probably be in a wheelchair, rather than on crutches.

I leaned my bike against the sign and switched from cycling clip-on shoes to my flip-flops, which looked funny with my neon-orange socks. Mason socks, as I called them. I looked around, hoping to see him or Stella coming toward me.

The minutes dragged on.

I watched other riders connecting with their families, and looked around for Rocco, our driver, or my mother, in case she'd ignored all my advice and come to meet me anyway. But I didn't see anybody I knew.

"Any sign of Stella?" asked Cameron, walking back from the water dispenser.

"Nope." I grabbed my bike bottle and drank some water. "I guess they didn't make it after all."

"Too bad, I really wanted to see her," said Autumn.

"Come on, guys—time to go get our group photo taken," said Margo. "We have to check in and then we get a pizza lunch. I think we even get ice cream."

"I will kill for ice cream," I said, and we headed over to

the pavilion, where Heather and Fred were checking in and congratulating all the groups. We each got a T-shirt that said I Helped Cure Cancer with the name and dates of the ride on the front, and Official Rider on the back. They were bright orange, like my Mason socks.

It was a look. Not a good one, but I loved it anyway.

Heather gave us an extra shirt to give to Stella and made us promise to deliver her best wishes.

We had our official picture taken, arms draped over one another's shoulders, Oxendale in the middle like the peak of a mountain range.

There we were, eight strong, spelling out ♥STELLA!

Maybe it didn't matter to Stella—at all. But it mattered.

When we were nearly home early that evening, after spending a few hours in Boston just hanging out, and then making the three-hour drive home, Elsa suddenly announced from the back seat, "We need to sign each other's shirts!"

"You're right—we should," said Margo.

We passed the shirts around, trading them back and forth, signing and writing funny or inspiring messages with the small set of Sharpies I'd brought just in case I wanted to draw. I drew pictures of people on bikes going up hills; of the Devil's Drop; and a portrait of Scully on Max's. The last hour or so of the trip went so quickly that I was surprised when the van pulled up in front of my house.

I almost thought Stella would be waiting there. But she wasn't. I got out as if I were in a daze. I was actually home. I tossed my autographed T-shirt on top of my bike helmet and duffel.

"See you around, Blondie," said Max as he wheeled my bike over to the garage. "Don't be a stranger."

"I won't. Besides, we'll always have that night with Scully," I said.

"What?" He laughed.

"Never mind," I said, and he gave me a big hug, nearly lifting me off the ground.

"Group hug!" Oxendale shouted, and everyone clambered out of the van and surrounded us.

Well, everyone except Max's uncle Rocco, our driver. That would have been weird. "I *hate* group hugs," said Cameron.

"You're not the only one," Margo added, reluctantly joining the huddle in our driveway.

"I'm going to see you guys at school on Monday," I said, laughing.

"So? It won't be the same," said Elsa. "We all know it."

As soon as we released the hug, Cameron hauled his bike out of the trailer, too. He slung his duffel over his shoulder. "I can take it from here," he said. "I don't live far. Just . . . over there. See you!" he called, and he started walking away as everyone else boarded the van.

Rocco beeped the horn a few times as they drove away, and I waved at the van, as if I needed to say good-bye to it, too.

"Hey, Cameron. Don't run off like that," I said, following him.

"I couldn't risk another group hug," he said. "You understand."

I nodded. "Yeah. I do."

"See you on the road." Cameron swung his leg over the bike and rode off, wobbling under the weight of his stuff.

CHAPTER 19

When my mother got home from the supermarket fifteen minutes later, she was disappointed to have missed my official return. But she gave me a giant hug and declared it "Your Favorite Dinner" night. While I took a shower, she made everything that I loved, things I'd missed during the trip. She kept commenting on how I looked healthy and athletic, but inside I felt terrible. I knew I was breaking her heart by not eating everything she made, but the truth was, I couldn't. I was just too exhausted. I had zero appetite, but I kept moving the fork to my mouth as if it would help.

"You seem preoccupied," Mom commented after a while.

"Did you see Stella today, or have you talked to her since you got back?"

I shook my head.

"Do you want to take the car and run over to her house? It's okay with me," she said. "I can imagine you don't want to ride your bike for a few days."

"Yeah. I don't know. Maybe the opposite," I said. "The bike and I got pretty attached."

"Well, how do you think she's doing? I haven't heard from her parents, which is odd," she said. "We're usually in touch about anything regarding you two."

I bit my lip. "I don't know how she is, not really. Every time I try to talk to her, she doesn't want to talk."

"She needs time. It's understandable. And you—look at what you just accomplished. You're exhausted right now. It's making it harder to deal with," Mom said. "But trust me, you guys will be fine."

"Oh, so when I'm all rested up, it's going to be easy?" I snapped. "Sorry, Mom. I—I need to be by myself right now."

I was home, and nothing had changed—yet at the same time, everything had changed.

I unpacked my duffel bag, dumping all the dirty clothes into the laundry basket, one by one, and then in bunches.

The bikini top fell out of one clump of clothes and dropped to the floor. I picked it up and slammed it into the wastebasket. I wouldn't be wearing that again. It reminded me of pain.

I reached into the bag to see what was left. A random half-eaten Luna bar and a packet of Gatorade powder. Another Sharpie pen. My phone charger.

There was one more thing I needed to do: clean out the bike's saddlebag, so I could be officially done with this trip. I went downstairs and out to the garage. Seeing the bike already made me feel emotional. Now what? It was a hand-me-down from Stella, something to make it possible for me to do the ride. Now I felt really attached to it. Would I have to give it back to Stella, or . . .

It's just a bike, a thing, I told myself. *Don't let it get to you.*

I walked over and unclipped the small saddlebag, which was heavy with tools. As I tilted it to one side to pull out the patch kit that Mason and his dad had made for me, my phone tumbled out and hit the cement floor—facedown. I'd forgotten it was in there.

Something else fluttered to the floor. A folded-up green piece of paper that was well worn and creased.

I picked both up. I was dreading seeing a cracked screen, but when I finally braved a look, my phone was fine. I unfolded the list. I wanted to take joy from accomplishing it.

I wanted to feel proud. But I didn't, because it wasn't mine to begin with.

I sat on the garage stoop and broke down crying, clutching the list and wishing, more than anything, that the last month hadn't happened.

I heard the door from the kitchen open, and my mom sat down on the step just below me, reaching up to hug me so that I could lean on her and collapse. We must have sat like that for five minutes. I was gasping and sobbing, my gut aching with exhaustion, relief, and sorrow for Stella.

When I stopped crying, my mom let go of me and told me to go upstairs and get ready for bed. "Give yourself a break. You've been doing everything lately, and you need some time."

I went back upstairs and took another long, warm shower. All I wanted was to sink into my bed and sleep. I'd figure out a better way to deal with all this tomorrow, I'd reach out to Stella again first thing in the morning, but right now, my body craved sleep more than anything.

I had dozed off when my phone rang. I reached up to grab it, nearly knocking it onto the floor. Stella's ringtone. I hadn't heard it in a long time. I managed a quick, desperate "Hello?" as I struggled to sit up in bed. I glanced at my alarm clock. It wasn't even nine yet. I was beat.

"Hey. It's me," Stella said.

"I know," I said. I grabbed the water bottle beside my bed and took a quick sip.

"I'm sorry I didn't come to see you finish."

"That's okay," I said. "I probably shouldn't have asked."

"No. It's *not* okay, actually. As you would say."

I waited for her to keep going. Lately, whenever I tried to talk to her, I only upset her by saying the wrong things.

"I've been acting horribly toward you. I know that, and I'm sorry," she said. "It wasn't fair of me to demand that you keep my situation a secret. I wanted more time, but you know, there isn't going to be a perfect time to tell people. I need to do it and move on. I realized that when I was sitting home wishing I'd gone to see you guys."

"All the same, I didn't plan to tell anyone your secret. I just kind of broke down," I said. "Which probably comes as no surprise to you, but I was really being as tough as I possibly could. I didn't say a thing to anyone for the longest time. It got harder and harder."

"You know what? I wish it could have been different. I wish I could have gone with you," she said. "The fact that I couldn't—the reason I couldn't—it just made me resent you. Constantly."

"I went because I thought you'd want that," I said. "You'd hate it if I gave up or gave in because of something that happened to you. Wouldn't you? You kept insisting I do the ride in the first place. And I even . . . I don't know if you're going to like this, but I have to tell you. I even did your F-It List. I wanted to surprise you. I wanted to give you something fun to think about or possibly even get you to laugh again."

She didn't say anything at first, and I started to panic. *Don't say so much, Frances. Let her talk,* I told myself.

"The thing about laughing is that . . . it's hard to do when you're alone," she said slowly. "When you feel all alone. Like there's nobody else in the world going through what you are. Like nobody else will ever get it. But I know—logically—that's not true. I don't have things that bad. There are lots of people suffering even more. Way more. You know? So then I get down on myself for being so self-centered and whiny. I don't—that's not normal for me."

"Yeah, but . . . nothing's normal right now."

"Except the *new* normal," Stella said. "Don't forget about that."

We had a history teacher who, whenever she was summing up a major historic event, would say, "And over time, the people learned to adjust to . . . the new normal." Stella and

I both recited it now, from memory, then started laughing.

"So, um . . . are we okay?" I asked. "Can I come visit you tomorrow?"

"Actually, I need you to pick me up, in the morning. Can you get your mom's car?"

"I'll try. What are we—where do you want to go?"

"You'll see. Good night, Franny."

"Good night, Stells. What time should I be—"

She hung up before I had a chance to press further. But that was okay. We'd made a start.

CHAPTER 20

When I walked into her house Sunday morning, Stella was in a wheelchair.

She was wearing a couple of layered T-shirts over a pair of shorts, and her damaged leg, which now ended above her knee, was wrapped in a few layers of beige ACE bandages. Cheeto was perched in the wheelchair beside her—mangy old Cheeto, whom she'd thrown across the hospital room a few weeks back.

Stella's shiny brown hair fell over her shoulders, looking almost the same as it always did—there were some wispy strands that she would need to grow out. But the bandages were finally gone from her face, and the superficial wounds she'd gotten had all but disappeared.

She looked like she usually did, for the most part.

"Wow. You look great," I said, amazed at how much she'd changed in a week.

"You were only gone for a week," she replied.

"I know," I said. "But you look better."

"Meanwhile, you've changed completely. What—your hair. Did you bleach it?"

"Kind of," I said. "I mean, yes."

"I like it."

"It's impossible to comb out for some reason. And Max wouldn't stop calling me 'Blondie,' which is highly tacky."

"He's like that. But he's nice, right?"

I thought of all the help and support Max had given me over the past week. "He's very decent," I said. "Although he always has to try to hook up with someone, which can drive you crazy after a while."

"Speaking of which, *I'm* going stir-crazy. Get me out of here already," she said.

I unlocked the wheelchair's wheels, and after Stella had a quick chat with Mrs. Grant about how long we'd be gone—I still had no idea where she wanted to go—we headed out the door.

The Grants had had a short ramp constructed while I was gone, and Stella easily—at least it seemed so to me—wheeled herself down it and over to my mom's car. I carefully helped her into the passenger side, sliding her over from the chair.

"I can use crutches, you know," she said. "Want to go back and get those instead of that bulky chair?"

"This is fine. Besides, your mom might not let us go if she thinks about it too long," I said. "Do up your seat belt."

I opened the trunk, prepared to store the wheelchair inside. A puff of peach fabric was taking up the whole right side of it. I pulled, and out came the ridiculous curtain dress I'd been trying on when I got the call about Stella, way back when. I had torn the bottom some, so it was nonreturnable. Still, I needed to go to Flanberger's at some point and settle up with Phyllis. I was surprised she hadn't tracked me down yet, but maybe she'd forgotten the incident. I'd been trying to, myself.

I grabbed the dress, which still had its tags attached, and stuffed it into the backseat to make room. Then I collapsed the wheelchair—I'd done the same with my grandfather's a few times—and put it in the trunk.

When I got into the car, it felt a little odd to be sitting beside Stella's changed body, but not all that different. "So, where do you want to go? Dunkin' Donuts? Somewhere else for coffee? I know a place where I can get you a sweet discount on hash browns," I joked.

"No, I'm not hungry," Stella said.

"Oh. Well, what did you have in mind?" The fact that she wanted to get together was good enough for me; I didn't care what we did or if we did anything at all.

"I need you to take me there," she said.

"Where?"

"You *know* where. The spot. The place," she said.

"Stells. Are you talking about . . ."

"Exactly. I have to see it," she said. "And why are you driving like an old lady? Are you worried you're going to break me or something? I'm fine."

"I haven't driven in a week—I don't know," I said. "I've never been good at driving and talking."

"True," she said. "You tend to miss turns and major exits. Just take Concord Street to 12 to 91 and slow down when we get to the dairy farm. I'll recognize the bend in the road when we get closer."

"Are you sure?" I asked.

"Yes. I've asked my parents and they keep putting it off," she said. "My dad told me there are cards and flowers marking the spot. Even now. A month later. Can you believe it?"

"I guess—I haven't been past there either," I said. I hadn't been going out of my way, exactly, but I had a vague idea of the location and I'd avoided it, unintentionally or not.

"That was such a beautiful day. Remember?" she said, tapping her fingers on the top of the door. She'd rolled down her window, so I opened mine, too, and popped the sunroof on my mom's Honda. "I got out of my last class early because the sub never showed up. I took off as fast as I could. Wait—slow down. I think that's it, up ahead."

I gently put on the brakes and glanced in the rearview mirror to see if anyone was coming up behind us. Nobody was, so I slowed down even more and pulled over onto the gravel shoulder. I didn't get far enough over on my first attempt, so I backed up and straightened out the car, making sure I left plenty of room for cars to safely pass us.

I turned off the engine and we sat there, staring straight ahead, at a bizarre little display of items: a very large pink teddy bear, a pile of other stuffed animals, bouquets of flowers both real and fake, a big piece of poster board covered with messages, a bike pump stuck in the ground like a flagpole.

We sat there for a few minutes, saying nothing, just watching cars go by us, hearing their engines zoom, their tires humming on the pavement. The air outside smelled as ripe as a cow pasture can smell in spring.

"Why?" Stella said. "That's what I keep asking myself."

"Why . . . would people leave flowers way out here?" I asked.

"No. Why was I *there* right then? Why didn't I move over more? What was wrong with that driver? I mean, they say it wasn't her fault, in the accident report. It was nobody's fault."

"I'm sure it wasn't *your* fault. It doesn't make sense—it's one of those random wrong place, wrong time things—"

"It has to make sense, Franny. Everything ultimately has to make sense." She opened the car door and started to pull herself out. She was balancing on one foot.

I raced around the car and offered my arm, and she put hers around my shoulder. She'd take one step, then we'd swing through the next step together. Just like when someone was injured at dance.

"People go nuts wanting to say they're sorry for other people. But it just makes everyone look at the accident place over and over. What good does that do? It's just a *place*," Stella said.

"But it's a place where something pretty awful happened. Maybe this could warn people, in the future?" I offered.

"Then we'll get a highway sign put here. 'Dangerous Curve Ahead' or 'Share the Road.' That'll be a little more helpful than a Beanie Baby." She frowned at the jumble of assorted mementos on the ground in front of us. "I don't want to leave anything here. I want it to be gone. As long as it's still here, it's like I'm stuck at that moment. Like my life ended. And it didn't."

"Then let's get rid of it. I can bag it up. Let's get you back to the car first, though."

"Do you think I could sit here for a second?" asked Stella.

"On the side of the road? I don't know. And what about getting up?"

"I have arms, silly."

I helped her sit just off the gravel, on the grass even farther over, so her bare legs wouldn't get scraped. Then I jogged back to the car and got two reusable shopping bags from under the front seat. I started gathering the flowers, stuffed animals, and everything else.

Stella sat in the grass, absentmindedly touching the blades with her fingers, running her hands back and forth. Apparently she hadn't been allowed to spend too much time outdoors over the past several weeks. She was desperate for fresh air and green grass.

"Franny. Franny! Look at this."

I stopped filling the bags and turned to her. She was holding up a small piece of metal. "What?" I asked, walking closer.

"It's part of my bike. It's half of my light—it's the inside of the light. Holy crap. How would you even—make that happen?" She suddenly started to cry. To sob.

I sat down and put my arm around her shoulders, and she leaned against me. We probably sat there for fifteen minutes, just like that, while cars went past, slowed, gawked at us, as if an accident had just happened.

"You girls okay?" a milk truck driver called to us.

"Fine!" I shouted back.

"Nothing to see here," said Stella, and we started giggling all of a sudden. "It's like they've never seen someone sit on the ground before. What is *wrong* with people?"

Back in the car with the bags of mementos stashed behind my seat, I handed Stella my mom's tablet, which had the slide show cued to begin. After I'd heard from Stella the night before, I'd stayed up late getting photos from everyone. Elsa and Cameron had come over and helped me edit it into a slide show of epic proportions—with sound effects, music, and labels.

Now, as Stella hit play, the whole trip began to spill out, from the first horrible ride in the van to Oxendale's awkward dancing, to my posing for a toast with Scully, and my attempts to start a food fight.

"You really did do my list," she said slowly. "That's why you bleached your hair."

"Seemed important to you," I said. "And I needed something to do besides be last."

During the piercing scene, suddenly the screen view slammed sideways and went black.

"That's when Mason fainted," I said.

"Why was Mason there?" she asked.

"Oh. Well, I needed a ride in order to get to the tattoo place," I said. That was true, but that wasn't why he'd been there. But we were doing so well; I didn't want to go into that story. I didn't want to rush things too much.

"Why couldn't you just go on your bike?"

"Because I'm not you!" I said.

Stella was laughing, snorting, gasping with surprise when she saw us all balanced on the lobster boat sculpture. While she couldn't hear us yelling, I'd added a caption that spelled out STELLLLLLLLLLLLA!

"I hate that play, movie, whatever," she said. "I hate Tennessee Williams for writing it, and I hate Marlon Brando for being good and making it a thing you have to watch in school."

"At least you're not named Blanche," I said. "'Cause she gets the worst of it."

"If I never read that play again, it'll be too soon," Stella muttered.

The slide show ended with the scene of all of us saying good-bye and signing our shirts.

"This ride looks like it was completely out of control," Stella said.

"No, it—well, was it? I don't know. I've never done it before."

"Can't say that anymore," Stella reminded me. She let out a loud sigh. "I'm actually glad everyone knows. I couldn't stand pretending anymore. And it's not like I can hide the fact that I'm going to be . . . you know."

"So what's the plan?" I asked. "For your leg."

"They have these amazing prosthetics with computers now. I mean, it won't be the same. But it's—you know, I'll be able to walk again. It's going to take time. It's a ton of work. That's the thing they keep warning me about. How hard it is."

"Good thing you like work. And good thing summer's coming. I've got nothing but time," I said.

"Yes, but you're not a physical therapist."

"No. But I can come with you every day," I said. "I can even drive you."

"Good point," she said. "I guess I will need some help. For a while. Until I get used to the new normal."

We both groaned. "Did you really just say that?" I asked.

"We'd better get going," Stella said, "before my mom and dad panic."

"Let's drive a little bit farther," I said. "We can call and tell them everything's fine."

"What did you have in mind?" Stella asked as I started the car and checked my mirrors before pulling back onto the road.

"I don't know. Let's just drive for a while. I haven't really seen you in, like, a month. We have some catching up to do. So, I was wondering," I said. "Do you think I did everything on the F-It List the way you meant?"

"I'm not sure. I might have to watch the slide show a few more times," she said. "I might have to check with some people who were actually *there*, and not just take your word for it."

"Good. Because they'd love to meet up, anytime you're ready," I said. "We even have an extra shirt for you."

"I don't know. I've been getting fitted for my prosthetic leg. It's cool-looking, I'll give it that. But they say it takes a while to learn how to walk with it, even after all the adjustments and fittings and stuff. Plus you have to keep what's left of your leg strong, so I'm in physical therapy for that."

"It's a lot to take on. You'll get there, though. I have complete confidence. And we'll do the ride next year, you know," I said.

"We will," Stella said. "I haven't decided what kind of bike to get. Dad's researching it. I'm sure he'll buy the most expensive one. I'll probably be faster than you. Just a heads-up."

"Of course, that goes without saying. But in the afternoons, you'll ride beside me so that I finish. *That* goes without saying, too." I drove faster, pushing the accelerator, hitting sixty as the road straightened out.

I had opened the sunroof wider, and behind me, the peach dress was rippling in the wind, making an annoying sound.

Stella reached behind me and pulled the cascading ruffles of gauzy material up to the front seat. "What is this?" she asked.

"It's the stupid dress I was trying on at Flanberger's when you—when your dad called. I ran out of the store and—do you remember me standing in your hospital room with it on?" I asked.

"God, no. You didn't *buy* this, did you?"

"Not exactly," I said.

"So why do you still have it? And why does it feel like a curtain?"

"Phyllis said it was magical," I said.

"Phyllis has been working at that store since 1842," Stella said, and we both laughed.

She reached up, holding the dress in her hands, pushing

with her good leg, forcing the material through the sunroof. Before she could even let go, the wind grabbed the dress, sucking it into the air, and I watched it billow out behind us like a sail that had snapped loose from its mast.

Fly like you mean it, bad-luck dress.

"Looks like you need another prom dress," said Stella.

"Or not," I said. "Because were we really going to go, anyway?"

"Yeah. Of course we're going," she said. "Just not wearing that nightmare."

CHAPTER 21

"This isn't a date," Cameron said when I came out the garage door, walking my bike to the curb. He was dressed in a black vintage suit jacket with a white shirt, classic skinny tie, skinny jeans, and gray Converse sneakers.

"Nope," I agreed, carefully getting onto my bike.

"But we are riding into the sunset on bikes," Cameron pointed out, "wearing semiformal clothes, so some people could construe this as something completely different."

"They wouldn't do that," I said, "would they?" My long, striped, stretchy dress was going to get in the way of the pedals, so I cinched the bottom into a knot at knee length. The three-inch heels of my strappy shoes dangled off the back of the pedals, while I wore my beaded black mini purse across my body like the world's smallest messenger bag.

Even tonight, I had to wear a helmet. I knew that my hair would spring right back into a semi-decent style once I got to school and put a little water in it. My neck was bare, which felt odd as I started riding. This dress did not cover me nearly enough, I realized, with its tie at the back of the neck, open back, and the questionable lingerie I had on underneath. I needed one of those billowy scarves that I'd seen in prom photos, but getting the dress at the last minute had been hard enough. Overnight shipping had saved me.

"God, I hate prom. I hate anything resembling prom," Cameron complained as we rode down the bike path, front bike lights flashing. We were the only ones on the path, which I didn't mind. It meant we could ride side by side.

"You're making a huge sacrifice. I get it," I said. "But it's for Stella. Which is why I'm about to get bike grease on this dress, catch it in the spokes, then tangle my shoes in the pedals."

"I don't do prom."

"No, I don't either," I said. "Usually."

"Actually, I've never even been before, but I already know I hate it." Cameron laughed. "I don't even like looking at fashion spreads of formal wear, and this is like ten thousand steps above that."

"Why *would* you like it? It's a dance. And you don't dance," I said to Cameron. "As a rule."

"A very good rule, I might add."

We kept on pedaling to school. I'd thought Stella would be doing this tonight, not me. She was the one who'd planned for it.

Instead, I'd wanted to drive and pick up Stella, but Mom didn't want me to drive on prom night, afraid of the worst, and Stella's parents insisted on bringing her and on picking her up. It made sense. They'd offered to give me a ride, but since I was trying to make sure everyone on the bike trip team went to prom, I had to go this way in order to convince Cameron to go.

Ten minutes later we zipped into the high school lot, which had a large sign—Mighty Sparrows Parking Only—in our school colors. Invariably, pigeons were the birds that liked to sit on the sign, leaving their marks on the cars that dared to park directly beneath it when all the other spots were taken.

A few limousines idled at the curb by the gym entrance. Cameron and I coasted to the bike rack near it. I carefully scooted off my bike, undid the knot, and let my dress fall to its full length. Then I took off my helmet and shook out my hair before crouching down to lock my bike. I had just finished when I heard a familiar voice ask, "Frances? That you?"

"No," I said calmly, "it's not." I stood up carefully and faced Oscar. He was on his way into the gym, with a girl I didn't recognize hanging on to his arm. I wondered if there was a way I could take her aside and warn her about Oscar, without ruining her night. Probably not.

Oscar laughed. "You biked to prom? Who *bikes* to prom?" He gestured to Cameron with his chin. "Nice helmet hair."

"Shut up," Cameron replied. He held out his arm and I took it, walking into the building. I felt like a different person. I didn't care what anyone else said or thought. We handed over our tickets to a friend of Margo's on the prom committee, and I briefly wondered where Margo was. Then I ducked into the bathroom to fix my hair and check my makeup. I was wearing more than usual, and I needed to put on a fresh coat of lipstick.

When I came out, Cameron was waiting for me. "Dude, I can't walk in there *alone*," he said.

We paused as we walked below an archway of balloons. "This feels familiar," I said.

"Should we get our picture taken?" he asked as we passed the portrait setup, with its fake-looking outdoor backdrop and giant school logo.

"Nah," I said. "We can get better pictures on our own." If Stella did show up, I might get my picture taken with her, I thought.

Once inside the gym, we nearly sprinted to the refreshments table for punch. On our way, I spotted Elsa dancing with friends. Beside her, Oxendale was jumping up and down, or what he called "dancing."

Cameron pointed to a banner on the wall, with the junior class prom theme printed on it: Embrace the Future, Today. "This is so awful." He looked miserable. I almost wanted to tell him to go ahead and go home, but not yet.

"It's pretty bad," I agreed.

"Embrace the future. I'm not embracing anything," Cameron said. "Or anyone, actually. How about 'No Group Hugs, Starting Now!' Could that be our theme?" he asked.

We both started laughing, just as Margo walked briskly past us. I grabbed her wrist, and she spun around with an irritated look. "Oh. It's you guys!" she said, her expression softening a little.

"How's it going?" I asked.

"Good. You look really nice," she said, stepping back to take a look at my dress.

"Thanks. You too," I said. I didn't do hugs, but I reached over and gave her a quick one anyway.

"I have to straighten out something with the DJ. I'll be back," she promised, before she strode off toward the stage.

"Don't look now, but I think Max is here," I said, gesturing over Cameron's shoulder.

"Impossible. He hasn't been at a school event since sixth grade," Cameron said.

We both started laughing, and that was when our vice principal, Ms. Bonaventure, called everyone's attention to the stage for the prom voting announcements.

Naturally, Autumn and Alex were in the running. As they stood onstage, they made eye contact with me, Cameron, and the rest of the group, who had all gathered around us. Oxendale was throwing them the tallest thumbs-up ever when he suddenly moved over and stood beside me. "Stella's here," he whispered.

I made my way through the crowd, not being able to see at Oxendale sky level. Then, once on the edge, I glanced over at the balloon arch and saw Stella on the far side of it. She was on crutches, wearing the elegant black dress she'd bought way back when. She'd gone to a salon and had her hair styled into an updo. As I got closer, I saw that she was wearing one black sandal, and her crutches were decorated with black and red ribbons. Her makeup was perfect. You couldn't even tell her face had been scraped up or that she'd been in the hospital for several days. She looked amazing, actually.

Behind me, the nominees for prom king and queen were being announced. "Ready to go in?" I asked.

"No. Is everyone looking?" she asked. "Is this the part where you make your big entrance and they announce you, like in old movies?"

"Like . . . Miss Stella Grant, the Duchess of Sparrows-dale? No, they don't. It's just an obnoxious balloon thing," I said. "Everyone's on tiptoes trying to see who's going to win prom king and queen."

"Pfft," she puffed. "Like we don't already know. Come on, let's get in there while everyone's distracted."

"Sure," I said, but I paused just after we started in. "Hey, hold on a second. We're here. We should celebrate. You're the one who decided we were coming, back in February. The fact that we're here—whether we have a good time or not—it's thanks to you," I said.

"It's no big deal," she said.

I knew she didn't like to make a big deal out of victories. The point was to have them, not to talk about them. "Right. I know," I said. "But thanks. Now, let's find a table."

As we wove through the crowd to a table near the front, more than a few people glanced at Stella, and whether they noticed she was missing a leg or not, I couldn't tell. I didn't care, and I hoped Stella wouldn't, either. People smiled or waved or looked surprised to see her. The accident had been in the newspaper, of course, and she hadn't been back to school since. No doubt there had been lots of rumors.

We sat down and one by one Elsa, Cameron, Oxendale, Max, and Margo joined us at the table, each giving Stella a hug and eagerly talking to her about everything.

"Drum roll, please," Ms. Bonvanture said. "And now, announcing your prom king and queen . . . Autumn Daye and Alex Nelson!" she cried. She tended to get overly excited about school royalty and things like that.

"Big surprise," Stella commented.

"I'm shocked. Utterly shocked," said Cameron.

"They really *should* get a tandem bike," Margo commented as we watched Autumn and Alex step off the stage and prepare to dance.

But before they danced, they ran over to hug Stella. Autumn even started to take her sash off and hand it to Stella.

"Giving up your throne? Already?" Cameron teased.

"Please—I know you mean well, but please don't do any of that honorary royalty crap," Stella said. "I just want to sit here."

"Got it. No problem." Autumn nodded, looking relieved, almost. She slipped her sash back on, and she and Alex twirled away in the middle of the gym while we all looked on.

Well, all except for Oxendale. He headed out to join them. Apparently prom royalty was not a thing where he came from.

"He has a bike jersey on under his suit," I commented to Stella.

"No, that's a soccer jersey. Please. He knows his formal wear," Stella said. "You wish Mason was here so you could dance, don't you?"

"What?" I laughed. "No, not at all. Why would we want him to suffer?"

"Come on. I know what's going on." She gave me one of her classic *I'm onto you* looks.

"No, he's—he's too old for me."

"Don't be stupid. He's only two years older than you," she said. "You'll be eighteen this summer, anyway, before he's even twenty."

"I will?"

"Do I *always* have to do the math? Yes, you will," Stella said. "And even though it's pretty weird considering your history of endlessly giving each other grief, you guys seem to have something sort of . . . cute. I'm not sure how."

"I could say we spent a lot of time together lately. And that's true. But I think it started before then," I said. "I'm sorry. Is it too strange? Because we don't have to—"

"Do you seriously think I'd want to get in the way of your relationship?" Stella asked. "I know I haven't been peachy lately, but I want you to be happy."

"Okay. But don't call it a relationship. It's more like a relation . . ."

"Bike?" she suggested.

"I was going to say dinghy, but that sounds horrible. Relationdinghy." We both cracked up laughing.

"We have to stop meeting like this," Mason said when I climbed into the cab of his pickup truck an hour later. He'd put my bicycle into the back. "But nobody should have to ride their bike home from prom."

"Cameron is. Oxendale is," I said. "Of course, Oxendale's already dressed for it, and Cameron can't wait to get out of the gym."

"Would you rather go with them, then?" he asked. "I thought you texted me."

"I didn't," I said, sliding out of my high-heeled shoes. My feet were killing me. "Stella did."

"Oh?" Mason's left eyebrow shot up.

"Yeah, she used my phone while I was getting us punch. When I came back, she informed me you were picking me up in half an hour and that I couldn't even try to get out of it."

"You're disappointed?"

"No! Not at all." I scooted over to be closer to him on the bench seat as we drove out of the high school parking lot. "I mean, I didn't want to leave her there, but she said she was fine. She's having a great time."

"So . . . she knows about us," Mason said slowly.

"Oh, yeah." I nodded. "She says she's okay with it. And since she's plotting and scheming to get us together on my stupid prom night, I guess I'm going to believe her."

"Why is it *your* stupid prom night?" He braked at a stop sign and looked over at me. "By the way, you look incredible."

I glanced down at my dress, embarrassed. I didn't usually bare my shoulders, or wear anything this kind of . . . sexy. "Thanks."

"Huge improvement over that thing you wore to the hospital," he went on.

"It'd be impossible *not* to be," I said.

"It suits you," he said.

We were both looking at each other intensely, and I had that same kiss-me-now-or-I'm-going-to-explode feeling.

"Do you think we should move on from this stop sign sometime?" I asked.

"Maybe," he said. "Maybe not." He reached over and pulled me toward him, knocking my little purse off my lap and onto the floor. "Where do you want to go?" he said softly, twirling my hair around his finger while he kissed my neck.

"This is . . . here . . . this is good," I whispered.

CHAPTER 22

"Hey, I didn't think you were coming."

"Sorry. I got out of work fifteen minutes late," I said as I climbed off my bike. I quickly locked it to the rack outside Rocco's Ink Den. Since coming back from the trip, I'd been riding whenever I could. Sure, it wasn't fun riding my bike to work at six in the morning on the weekends, but I'd been through worse.

"You coming in?" I asked Mason, who was leaning against the front of his pickup, reading a book and looking extremely hot for a second there.

"What do you think?" he replied, squinting at me.

"You'll wait outside," I said, nodding. "That's probably a good idea."

"While you're out here, could you get me a hot mocha? With whipped cream?" Stella asked. "I might need to be revived after this whole thing."

"Frances? I'm apparently taking orders," Mason said. "What can I get you?"

"Iced tea," I said.

"Sure thing." Mason opened the truck door and tossed his book inside, then started walking down the sidewalk toward the small coffee shop next door to Flanberger's.

"He'll probably run into Phyllis," I said. Fortunately, my mom and I had gone in the Monday after prom and paid for the peach dress/curtain. Phyllis had given us her employee discount when I explained the whole thing.

"She'll try to sell Mason a dress," Stella said. "Poor Phyllis."

"Poor Mason," I added with a laugh. "So, you ready?"

"Let's go in."

I held the door and Stella walked in, using her crutches. She had her favorite boot-cut jeans on, with the one pant leg folded where her leg ended and pinned up to the back belt loop.

Max was working behind the counter.

Surprisingly, there was no tattooed girl or any girl at all hovering around him.

"Blon—Frances! Stella! I saw your name on the appointment list. Okay, first of all, you guys are not eighteen."

"Sure I am. In fact, today's my birthday, which is why I'm here." Stella reached into her pocket and pulled out the ID that had been delivered to her house the day before. What can I say? I owed Liam Herzog-Williams, and he was happy to do the job.

"Oh, yeah? Well, uh, happy birthday." Max walked around from the back of the counter, leaned down, put his hands gently on Stella to steady her, and kissed her. Hard. "Let me check with Rocco, make sure he's ready."

As he walked away, Stella brushed her lips, disbelieving. "I don't even want to know how many other girls he's kissed."

"No, you don't." I thought of the endless parade of girls I'd seen him with on the bike trip. "But was it good anyway?"

"It kind of was," Stella admitted.

"Let's call it epic. One item down on your list, nine to go," I said.

She looked over at me and smiled. "Great, now I have to live up to you? Oh, crap. This is going to hurt, isn't it?"

"I'll be here the whole time," I said as we followed Max to the piercing room, where Rocco was waiting for us.

11 People I Need to Thank:

1. Catherine Wallace, inspired editor of multiple drafts
2. Jill Grinberg, fabulous agent with history of riding "rolling hills"
3. Erin Downing, deadline enforcer
4. Janey Klebe, piercing expert
5. Kristin Pederson, keeping the crazy at a minimum
6. Maureen Sackmaster Carpenter, literary cyclist
7. Dawn Toboja, supporter extraordinaire
8. Amy Baum, pen-and-paper supplier
9. Wendy Scherer, riding ahead of me since Ocooch '95
10. Ted Davis, tire-changing expert
11. Cady Davis, because cuteness and "let's write!"

Turn the page to read

the first chapter of Catherine Clark's

How to Meet Boys

CATHERINE CLARK

Lucy

"Is this it?"

"This can't be it."

Mikayla and I climbed out of my car and stood in the gravel driveway.

It was June 10, our summer vacation had started two and a half days ago, and we'd just driven three hours from Minneapolis to stand outside what was supposed to be our dream house for the summer.

"The pictures your grandmother sent made it look a lot better," Mikayla commented.

I had to agree. The small cabin was painted dark red and had white shutters on a few of the windows—while a few other shutters were hanging off, and one had already fallen to the ground. Pine trees surrounded the house, not letting much sunlight through, and I noticed as I got closer that the paint was peeling in a few places.

The screen door practically came off its hinges when I opened it. I removed the envelope taped to the door, and inside was a short note from my grandparents, along with the house key.

WELCOME TO BRIDGEPORT! my grandmother had written in all caps.

We don't have a name for this place yet—hoping you girls will think of one as the summer goes on. We know the place needs a little work—we've given it a fresh paint job inside, and we'll help you find more furniture. We're excited to have you here!
XXOO Nana & G

"Should we go in?" asked Mikayla.

"I guess so. Here goes nothing," I said as I slid the key into the lock. It didn't work at first, so I rattled the doorknob a few times until the door swung open—*fell* open is more like it.

We walked into a narrow entryway beside a tiny coat closet. I flipped on the lights and saw the living room, dining room, and kitchen all in one glance. We wandered down a hallway that led to the bathroom and two bedrooms, one with two single beds and one with a double bed.

"Well, it's small," said Mikayla as we walked back out to the kitchen, "but it's cute small."

"My mother would call it 'cozy charm,'" I said, making air quotes. "Rustic cabin with authentic fireplace and huge heart. Massive potential!" I laughed, half at the house and half at the fact I was quoting my mother's real estate language.

Mikayla ran her fingers along the kitchen counter, which was made of some prehistoric tile material—in brown. "We can make it look better," she said. "We just need to invest in some cute accessories."

The small town where my grandparents live and have an apple orchard is in northern Minnesota. I love everything about Bridgeport, from its old-fashioned street signs to the lakeside cafés. I even love the slow-moving traffic, as long as I'm not the one driving in it.

But this house? I wasn't so sure.

I poked around the kitchen. My grandparents had furnished the place sparingly, with some dishes, a coffeemaker, a well-used toaster oven, and dish towels. In the living room there was a flowered upholstered chair that I remembered from my grandparents' porch—the faded material was a give-away—and two folding beach chairs, with an upside-down cardboard box for a coffee table and a couple of floor lamps that also looked like castoffs.

The rest was going to be up to us, or we could spend the summer living in what looked like the set from a depressing one-act play. That no one would ever go see.

There was no TV, but Mikayla and I both had our computers, so if we could ever get Wi-Fi here, we'd be set . . . but right now I wasn't counting on that. Instead, I figured I'd be doing a lot of reading over the summer, which was fine with me. I wanted to get ahead in a couple of my fall AP classes and be ready for the college-level courses I'd take in the winter and spring. Plus, there were college applications to think about, essays to write . . . Why did I suddenly get the feeling this was going to be an Abraham Lincoln summer? Me, a candle, a pen, some paper . . . and a brilliant speech that I could trot out when I became valedictorian.

Ha ha ha ha ha ha.

I usually visited every summer for a week or two, came on long weekends occasionally, and spent a few Christmas vacations here, when the bay would freeze and you could actually drive on it. But this summer, for the first time ever, I was moving here for two and a half months.

Mikayla and I were living completely on our own, but of course we'd had to swear on our lives to be responsible in every way, as if we weren't all the time anyway. We were practically saints, if you want to know the truth.

Of course, there was no rule that we had to behave exactly the same here as we did at home.

"Which is going to be my room?" asked Mikayla.

"I don't know." We stood in the doorways of each bedroom, surveying the spaces. "Do you want the bigger bed?" I asked.

"No, you take it," Mikayla said. She flopped onto one of the single beds. "Hey, this is pretty comfy."

I walked through the living room and onto the small deck off the back of the house. The view from there was incredible and explained why my grandparents had bought this place. You could see down to the harbor below. "Mikayla, come out here!" I called.

She hurried out the sliding door from the living room. "Now this is what I'm talking about."

"No, it's what *I* was talking about on the way up." I laughed. "My nana said, 'It's not much, but there's a view.' She was right on both counts."

We went back outside to start unpacking the car. The first thing we had to do was remove our bicycles from the car rack, and then take off the rack so we could open the back of my small SUV. Once we got that done, we hauled the boxes out of the back, along with a couple of suitcases of clothes and a few duffel bags.

"You want a ride to the beach club in a while?" I asked, as I carried a desk lamp in one hand and a blow-dryer in the other. "I want to go see my grandparents." Neither of us would start work for a few days—we'd wanted to get to town early and spend a few days settling into the place.

Mikayla set down a bag of oranges on the kitchen counter. "I think I'm going to go for a bike ride, visit the Club, and meet Sarah. I told her we were getting to town today and she said I could drop by for a tour. I could use the exercise after being in the car for so long. Plus, I need to make sure I can find the place, right?"

"You remember where it is, though," I said.

"Pretty much," she said. "It's the getting back *here* part I'm not sure about. Is this technically the woods, or the forest?"

I laughed. "You're such a city kid. It's Hemlock Hill Road. If you remember that, you can find your way back here. Look at the lake, and then head, you know, up the hill."

She squinted at me. "Are you making fun of me?"

"Maybe," I said.

"You're the one who almost got back on the highway heading the wrong direction," Mikayla said as she sorted things in the kitchen, putting away the small sets of plates and glasses she'd picked up at a Goodwill: some matched and some didn't, but they all looked really cool together. "Not me."

We both started laughing and she handed me a filtered pitcher to fill with water. "Can I help it if I get confused by lunch?" I said, running the cold water a bit. Suddenly the faucet made a loud clanking noise and went from running, to spraying randomly, and back to running smoothly again.

"This place is going to be interesting, isn't it?" Mikayla asked, eyeing the sink.

"Let's hope so," I said, wiping water off my forehead with my sleeve. "We didn't drive two hundred miles to be bored."

I was heading to the Apple Store later that afternoon when it happened.

Not *that* Apple Store, where customers line up outside whenever a new iPhone, iPad, or other cool iProduct is released. No, this was The Original Apple Store, which was owned by my grandparents and sold real apples. Crunchy ones. Tart ones. Sweet ones. McIntosh, Cortland, Haralson, Honeycrisp, Northern Spy, Prairie Spy, Rome, and so on.

My job wasn't to know the apples in stock. That was for whoever worked at the Apple Genius Bar. (My grandparents were hoping to get sued by Apple, for the free publicity. They even had a bumper sticker that said *iApple—Do You?* with their store logo on it. They're begging to be caught, and when they go to jail, I'll visit them. Hopefully the trial will be in California, where Apple is based, because I've always wanted to go there.)

Anyway, it's apples versus oranges.

Literally.

My grandparents go a little crazy with the decorations. One is an apple and an orange on different sides of a scale and the headline *You can't compare them—don't even try!*

My grandparents had hired me because they said they needed "reliable" help. Last summer's teen hires had been a disaster, so they'd started begging me as far back as last Christmas. When I resisted, they'd thrown in a house. (And by *house*, I mean that rundown cabin we'd just seen for the first time.)

My parents wouldn't let me live up here on my own, so I'd invited my friends Mikayla and Ava to come with me. Unfortunately, Ava's mother thought it was time for her to have a "serious" job that might help her get into college, so Ava had pursued a few internships and ended up with one at a fashion and arts magazine based in Chicago. I was happy for her, because she really wanted to be in a city—but I was disappointed she couldn't come up here to stay with me and Mikayla.

My grandmother had helped Mikayla find a job at the Bridgeport Beach Club. (When I asked why we couldn't work together at the Apple Store, Nana had said, "The two of you would have too much fun—you wouldn't get anything done.")

Mikayla definitely got the better deal. Not only did the Bridgeport Beach Club= pay more, but it was also a very cool place to work because of the big group of people our age working at the Club. I was probably crazy for *not* trying to get a job there. When I started smelling like apples, no doubt I'd regret the decision.

Still, the Apple Store was a lot better than what I did the summer before. I worked at the Mall of America in a coffee chain that had four locations inside the mall. The managers rotated us from store to store, like we were car tires that needed to be switched every ten thousand coffees.

You couldn't have a sharper contrast. I was going from listening to shrieking people on roller coasters and other neon-colored rides twisting upside down above my head— and I can't stand rides—and parking ramps as big as an entire city and endless levels of food courts . . . to this peaceful summer resort town perched on a bay beside one of the Great

Lakes. I took a deep breath of the fresh northern air.

Yes, I was going to enjoy this, I thought as I turned to enter the store.

As my foot hit the first step, someone walked out.

I looked up—and up and up, he was tall—and nearly tripped on the second step. It wasn't just any guy. It was Jackson Rolfsmeier. Sure, his hair was a little longer than the last time I'd seen him, and he was about six inches taller, but he was still the same boy I'd kissed, or tried to kiss, back in eighth grade, only to have him say, "Um, no," and run away. It felt like a century ago, but at the same time it could have been a couple of weeks, considering how nervous and embarrassed I felt even now, three years later.

Jackson was holding the door open for me, waiting for me to come in.

My pulse immediately doubled. Then tripled.

I hadn't seen Jackson up close in about three years, since the kiss incident and the rumors that floated around after it. Once or twice the summer before this one, I'd seen him in town, but I crossed to the other side of the street to avoid him. I was mature like that. But it just didn't make sense to make small talk.

We didn't hate each other. We just . . . well, it was awkward. The way it can be when you go through something really, really embarrassing with a person.

"Hi," he sort of grunted out of the side of his mouth. "Lucy."

It came out as two different thoughts, like he couldn't combine the two. He could say "Hi" and he could say "Lucy," but not together. That might break some unwritten law boys had about acknowledging girls.

I looked up at him. Since when did he have a low voice like that? He sounded like he could do voiceovers for a movie trailer.

He had the same brown hair but it was longer, reminding me of a scruffy Liam Hemsworth. As I stepped up, I realized he had a good half foot on me, height-wise. When did he get so tall? I wished I weren't at such a height disadvantage for such an awkward conversation.

"Oh, hey," I said, pushing my hair back with my hand, the way my mom is always saying I shouldn't do because it's "a tic." Tic, schmick. My hair gets in my eyes sometimes. I didn't have anything else to say, really. My brain was too busy trying to figure out why this had to be the first thing that happened this summer. It felt like a bad omen. *Um, you haven't talked to me in three years. And I haven't talked to you, either. Why are you even saying hi? Did something fall on your head?*

So I just walked into the store and Jackson let the door close behind me, and he went on his way, and I was in the store and that was that.

Except . . . there was something I realized as the door closed.

Jackson was wearing an Original Apple Store staff T-shirt, which could mean only one thing. We were going to be working together.

We're going to be working together. This was the other so-called responsible teen my grandmother had found? *Him?*